HIS
HOUSEKEEPER
BRIDE

HIS HOUSEKEEPER BRIDE

BY

MELISSA JAMES

First published in Great Britain 2009
Large Print edition 2010
Harlequin Mills & Boon Limited,
Eton House, 18-24 Paradise Road,
Richmond, Surrey TW9 1SR

© Lisa Chaplin 2009

ISBN: 978 0 263 21187 0

Harlequin Mills & Boon policy is to use papers that are
natural, renewable and recyclable products and made
from wood grown in sustainable forests. The logging and
manufacturing process conform to the legal environmental
regulations of the country of origin.

Printed and bound in Great Britain
by CPI Antony Rowe, Chippenham, Wiltshire

To the woman who inspired this book
with an extraordinary life: I am privileged to be
your friend. You raised a family from the age of eight,
survived the worst horror a young girl can imagine,
and yet you're constantly giving.
You have no idea how special you are.

To Vicky, a woman of true giving, strength and
compassion: you don't even know how you inspire
others as you do what needs to be done.

To my beloved Mia: thank you for loving these
characters, and never giving up on this book.
My friend, my sister, we're always a continent apart,
yet our friendship goes from strength to strength.
Remember you are never as others define you;
you are what your heart is, loving and giving.

My deepest thanks go to my dear friends and
CPs Robbie, Barb and Rachel, particularly Rachel,
for showing me where and when I wandered off track,
and Barb, for taking the time to read for me while
on retreat. Special thanks to Nikki for reading
at short notice. I thank you all.

PROLOGUE

St Agatha's Hospice, Sydney, fifteen years ago

THERE she was again, standing just outside the window, giving him her sweet smile, her little encouraging wave. His friend with the sunny red-gold curls, big brown eyes and brave, dimpled smile that made her look like Shirley Temple.

She was in the copse of trees and flowering shrubs in the middle of the hospice that she called the garden. The secret garden, she called it—named for her favourite book, which she read over and over to herself, as well as to her little brothers.

It was her escape from a reality and a future even grimmer than his.

She was his escape. They'd met only in the confines of this hospital during the times her mother's and Chloe's hospitalisations coincided, yet she *saw*, understood him, as his family no longer did. Sometimes he felt as if he was standing in a black and blinkered place, screaming for help, but surrounded by people who saw only Chloe's needs, who were tuned only to Chloe's voice.

Except for this thirteen-year-old girl who knew almost nothing about his life—a girl he never saw unless he was here. 'Shirley Temple' was his light and warmth in a dark, cold world, his colour and life. Everything had faded to black or white except for her.

Mark waved back at her, letting her know he'd join her soon. Their brief exchanges of maybe twenty minutes made her day bearable, just as they did his. They talked, or didn't talk; it didn't matter. It was the only time in the day when she wasn't playing the adult, and when he actually felt like the kid he still was.

He glanced briefly back inside the room, but everything in there was a blur of white, a deathly shade of pale. The blankets, the walls, the gown Chloe wore, her face—even the blue oxygen tube going into Chloe's nostrils—had somehow faded into the pale thinness of her. Beneath her knitted pink cap her hair was in a plait, roped over her shoulder, thin and dull. Even shining with lipgloss her mouth looked defeated, transparent.

Her eyes were like a delicate cobweb on a winter morning, rimed with frost. Broken with a touch. She was *sixteen*, and she was dying....

He was seventeen, and he was watching his best friend die—just as he'd been watching it for five endless years. Chloe had turned from childhood pal to his lover and bride of four weeks, and, watching her, he wanted to scream, to punch holes in the walls, to bolt as far away from this place as he could.

Oh, help—that sounded so *selfish* when he'd loved her almost all his life! But part of him felt as if *he'd* begun to die too when she'd got cancer, or as if he was chained to a cage: he wasn't *in* the cage but he couldn't fly away, either—and the only person who understood how he felt was a thirteen-year-old kid.

Carrie and Jen would be here in five or ten minutes. Chloe's best friends came every day after school, to tell them who was dating who, who'd broken up with who, and how ugly it had got. About the fight between Joe Morrow and Luke Martinez over who'd lost the opening game of the football season, and '—*don't choke*—Principal Buckley is getting *married*—like, at forty. How gross is that? He's so *old*.'

When Carrie and Jen came, Mark took off for a while. It was his time to breathe, to *be*. Chloe would fill him in on the Big News after. It gave them something to talk about.

Waiting for his escape time, he let his gaze touch all the reminders of life and normality. There was the massive Get Well card—as if she had a choice—signed by the whole school—even old Buckley and Miss Dragon-face Martin; the flowers-and-hearts and stick-figure finger paintings by Katie, his six-year-old sister, and Jon, Chloe's eight-year-old brother; the flowers his other sisters Bren and Becky picked for Chloe every day…

There was also a photo of Chloe, Jen and Carrie in a group hug, from when their school year had gone to the Snowy Mountains. Clear-skinned, tanned and laughing, Chloe looked so beautiful and healthy—as if nothing could hurt her. He remembered her smell that day. Like wind and sunshine and smiles. To her, it had been as if taking a six-hour trip on a bus was Everest and she'd conquered it.

It was the last time she'd gone out with her class.

As he stood by the bed he kept trying to calculate when he'd last had a day not spent in hospital, or at a doctor's office or thinking about illness and death. It was all a blur—as if he was a slow car stuck on a fast freeway. Everyone else around him rushed and flew, while he chugged along, unable to go faster. Just waiting.

It was a sunny day outside, a soft spring afternoon, perfect for testing the capabilities of his new motorised go-cart. But he was stuck in this room, watching the life drain out of Chloe, and there was *nothing* he could do about it.

'Prof…? Prof?'

The pain lacing her voice tore at his guts, but Mark couldn't make his head lift. The girl in the bed—strained, so thin, the hollows beneath her eyes the biggest and most colourful part of her—wasn't his best friend. This girl had given up. Secondary cancer had gone from her bones to her lungs, and finally her brain. It was over—apart from the endless *waiting*.

'Come on, Prof, look at me.' Chloe's thready voice gained strength by that hard-headed will of hers—the same will that had talked him into playing with her when they were four and he'd hated girls. The same stubborn faith that had made her believe he'd marry her one day—she'd been saying it since they were five—and had seen her become his research partner in the inventions he made in his backyard workshop. The same adorable persistence that had given him acceptance at school when the other kids had thought his flow of ideas strange and stupid. Because Chloe had believed in him, because beautiful, popular Chloe Hucknall had said she was going to marry Mark Hannaford, he'd become part of the inner circle.

'I know you hate looking at me now, but I wouldn't ask if it weren't important.'

He didn't hate it—or her—but he hated what she was about to ask, what he knew she'd say. Because she'd been asking the same thing for days—for weeks now. He felt like a sleepwalker bumping into the same wall over and over.

He'd turned seventeen five weeks ago. Last time he'd looked he'd been twelve, asking what osteosarcoma was and when was Chloe getting better, because he had this *massive* idea he needed to work on with her. Then the days and years had become like potatoes under a masher. Though he'd gone to school and found a part-time job, got his learner's permit and his driver's licence, had worked hard and passed all his exams, created things for her to marvel at or give ideas for im-

provement, this place, this *pain*, was all that
was real.

'Mark—*please*. I need you.'

I need you. The words he'd answered from the
time she'd roped him into fixing her Barbie doll
after Milo Brasevic had ripped its head off. He
felt encased in darkness, with dark shutters fallen
over his soul, yet he made himself look at her, and
from somewhere deep inside he even forced a
smile. It felt weak and hollow, but he managed
it—for her, his best friend, the girl he'd loved
ever since he could remember.

'Yeah? Whaddya want, Slowy?'

Mark and Chloe—the Mad Professor and
Slowy. Always had been, always would be.

Chloe's answering grin was weak, but her thin,
pale face was radiant with the love she'd never
tried to deny in all the years they'd known each
other. 'You didn't promise yet, George.' For no
reason he'd ever known, she called him George
when she was trying to be funny. 'I swear, I won't
die until you promise,' she joked, her eyes glis-
tening with tears of cheated wishing for all the
years they'd never have together.

'Then I'll never do it,' he replied huskily.

Chloe stopped smiling. 'Stop it, Mark. It

doesn't help—and I'm so *tired*. I know you're not gonna do so well without me, but you have to promise…' She closed her eyes, but the tears kept squeezing through. 'Don't spend all your time going for a scholarship, or hanging out in your shed alone with your inventions. You—you have to find another girl to love when you grow up, have kids…'

What was he supposed to say to that? *Yes, dear*? He knew how much it cost her to keep on asking day after day, because he couldn't *stand* to think of another guy touching her even if he'd been the one lying in that hospital bed.

Chloe was dying, and he had to live the rest of his life without her.

The bile rose hard and hot and fast, like a burning catapult. He turned and stumbled out of the ward—he wasn't going make it to the bathroom.

He made it outside the swinging doors, past the metal garbage can, and ran through the first door—the one leading to the tiny walled-in garden—before the sickness hit.

His hands and legs shook so badly he couldn't make his knees or his feet work. His breathing hurt, and there was a burning pain all the way up his chest and throat—but it was better than going back and having Chloe see him like this.

He knew that she'd try to force him to give the promise—or get their parents to talk to him again. *Give her the promise, Mark. Do it for Chloe.*

The same words he'd been responding to for five years—from going with her to her specialist appointments, to going back to school, to marrying her in a hasty backyard ceremony a few weeks ago.

Sometimes he just wished he'd *had* a choice to make. He'd like to know he'd have done all he had *without* the family's persuasive tactics.

'Here,' came a sweet, piping voice from behind him.

Mark's voice was croaky as he realised she was there. 'Hey, Shirley Temple.'

He liked calling her that as much as he liked the fact that she never used his name. If they didn't say Mark and Mary this wasn't real, it wasn't happening to them…and without names their shared time seemed a harmless dream, far from grim reality.

She was holding out a wet flannel to him. Crouching on the path beside him, she seemed luminous as the sun dipped behind the wire fencing at the end of the garden and framed her reddish-blonde curls. He knew those big fox-brown eyes of hers would be filled with the silent understanding only she could give. 'Put it on your face and your neck. It helps take the burning away.'

He took the cloth and wiped his face and throat. The pain eased a little. 'Thanks.'

'Keep it there.' She handed him a glass of water. 'Sip it slow.'

He nodded and sipped, and it eased the pain a little more. He felt it again—the unspoken connection. This pale, tired girl, looking so young until you looked in her eyes, felt like his only ally in a war he hadn't signed up to fight. 'Thanks.'

'You're welcome.' She reached out and touched his hand.

He could feel her hand shaking, could see her corkscrew curls bobbing with the effort to stay steady. 'Bad day?' he asked quietly.

She gave him a smile that wobbled. 'The doctor told us to say goodbye. Mum told me to be a brave girl and look after the boys.'

Oh, God help him. God help them both in what they had to face when they left here.

'Want to hit something with me?' he asked, to see what she'd do. Maybe she needed to lash out, to scream or yell, do *something* to let her suffering out.

She gave a gulping laugh, then two fat tears welled in her eyes. 'I have to set a good example for the boys.' Her slight body began to shake and lurch forward.

'Come here.' He held the trembling girl in his arms, feeling safe, at peace. She lived inside a similar cage to his, and she wasn't asking anything from him but to hold her, to understand.

Weird how a girl barely out of childhood could become his only haven...even weirder how he'd become hers, too. But he sure couldn't seem to make anyone else happy.

When she lay still against him, the only sound her hiccupping now and then, he wiped her tears with the cloth she'd brought for him. 'Hey, you want a drink or something?'

A soft, catching double breath told him she hadn't heard. Probably she'd spent the night caring for her youngest brother, who had croup.

Nobody knew the Brown family's story, for none of them talked about themselves. They all knew 'Shirley Temple' was the oldest of four kids. Local gossip said that Mrs Brown shouldn't have had the last of her children because she was too sick; she had something wrong with her heart that could threaten her life. She'd had him three years ago by C-section, and had been slowly dying since then, her heart too weak to pump. She'd been on the list for a transplant, but when one had finally come she'd been too sick for the operation.

So while Mr Brown was crying over the imminent loss of his wife, Shirley Temple was caring for the needs of her little brothers. It was the scandal of the hospital, but the girl did it all with a serene, defiant smile, neither complaining nor welcoming any sympathy. Social workers had come and gone, amazed by the strength of this girl who played a mother's part with seeming ease, refusing to admit she needed any help from the networks.

But she had to sleep some time…someone had to let her sleep. Poor kid.

His back was aching from sitting up unsupported. Holding her awkwardly in his arms, he wriggled back until he found the trunk of a big, thick old pine tree in the centre of the garden. He rested against it and closed his eyes, feeling a deep sense of life and hope emanating from her. Peace enveloped him.

'Mary! *Mary!*'

The panicked bellow woke them both with a

start. Mark peered around the darkening garden with bleary eyes. The last thing he'd remembered was yawning. Now the sun was behind the western wall. Dusk had come and was almost gone.

'Mary!'

'Shirley Temple' jumped in his arms; Mark let her go, and she scrambled to her feet, rubbing her eyes, still swaying with tiredness. 'Da-Dad?'

A man was peering out of the slide-up aluminium window on the opposite ward to Chloe's. He had that poleaxed look of grief that Mark had seen on too many faces in the past few years.

'She's gone.' He didn't even seem to notice that a strange boy was standing beside his daughter, had been holding her in his arms. 'She's gone, Mary.'

A child's cough and a wail came from inside the room behind him.

Mark watched 'Shirley Temple'—Mary— sway again, her lip tremble and her eyes blink. He waited for the tears to come. Then she squared her shoulders. 'I'm coming.'

Mark turned to stare at Mary's father. In disbelief he saw the man's face crumple with relief. 'You're my good girl…' He withdrew from the window.

Mark watched Mary walk away with a poise that seemed totally wrong. She was *thirteen* and she'd just lost her mother. How could she be so—so *calm*?

'Mary?' he said, using her real name for the first time.

Mary turned her head, looking over her shoulder at him. In that moment he saw not the girl but the woman she would become. No: there was a woman already inside her—a person of more courage and strength than he'd ever have. Her eyes were open windows to a beautiful soul—and Mark grieved for the maturing of this girl to a woman he'd want to know. Because this was the last moment he'd have with her. She was leaving—going to that unbearable future without him.

'Will you be—all right?' Inadequate words for all he wanted to say.

Her bottom lip was sucked under the top one, and tears were falling down her cheeks, but the delicate body was tight and straight. He saw the contours of her body in the silhouette of shadowy lights against the wall, the last light of the falling sun, and for the first time he saw a girl poised on the brink of womanhood. It was a reaction as physical as it was emotional, and guilt pierced him that he could even *think* that way when Chloe was in the room behind him, dying....

'I promised,' Mary said simply. 'Goodbye, Mark. I have to go now.'

And then she was gone.

Mark stood in the garden until darkness filled it. Then he walked back into the ward, to Chloe's room. The entire family was there, and each of them had identical expressions of grief and accusation on their faces as they looked at him—even Katie and Jon.

The tense, exhausted look on Chloe's thin face broke him. It was obvious she'd spent most of the afternoon fighting her wasting body, summoning up all her reserves of courage and strength to continue her quest for his promise. It meant that much to her to believe that one day he'd find happiness again.

He waved the family out with the cold fierceness that was starting to feel like a second skin over his heart and soul. 'I'll do it,' was all he said when they were alone.

Those cobweb-delicate eyes slowly closed; her face relaxed. She brought his hand to her cheek—the hand that had for four weeks borne his ring.

'Thank you,' she whispered, and drifted back into a ghost-like sleep, releasing his hand as her body unwound like a coil with its pressure released.

Mark's hand moved over her limp hair. Even now Chloe was beautiful, yet all he could see at this moment was the face of the girl who'd just left him behind. Perhaps because he saw a mirror of Mary's reflection in Chloe's acceptance of death, the dignity, grace and courage to say goodbye, to make a promise and keep it.

Filled with hatred at the thought of what he'd promised, Mark clenched his free fist and sat on the chair beside his wife's bed, watching her face. Waiting again…and already missing his only friend.

CHAPTER ONE

Office of the CEO, Howlcat Industries, Sydney Harbour, the present day

'WHY, Bren? Why the—?' Mark skidded to a mental halt, remembering his three-year-old niece was sitting on his lap. Shelby was prone to repeat anything he said and then bat her long golden eyelashes at her father when she got in trouble for it, saying, *'But Unca Mark says it.'* He amended his words. 'You think she'll do, so why do I have to interview this woman? She's a *housekeeper*. I have better things to do with my time than—'

Brenda Compton, née Hannaford, pulled her thick dark-blonde hair back off her face and fanned her neck, but grinned at Mark's careful pruning of his language. 'Well, of course, if you *want* me to conduct the interviews for you, find another…um…*suitable* woman…'

He set his jaw at the reminder. He might be CEO of Howlcat Industries, Australia's most successful engineering firm, in total control of the company he'd built from the ground up—but at home he had too many reminders of his humanity. His family knew him well, as no one else did—his hidden weaknesses, the way he spaced out when caught by an idea...

And they never failed to reminder him of the promise he still hadn't kept. But why had Bren chosen now, *today*, to make that reminder, to find him another *suitable* woman?

Today was his wedding anniversary. In six weeks it would be the anniversary of the day he'd become a widower.

His mother and his sisters had interviewed every housekeeper he'd ever hired. Before he gave them a contract he had them vetted by the best security firms in the country, and he paid them well. He also forced them to sign a confidentiality clause.

None of his precautions had stopped his employees selling their story about him to the tabloids, or bringing along their daughters or nieces, who happened to be pretty and single and, who'd love to be taken out on the town, marry a multi-millionaire and give him the family and kids his parents and sisters so romantically believed was in his future.

Today was a reminder that he'd *never* risk his heart and soul again. He'd never risk becoming a person so lost in grief that he'd almost—

Grimly he blocked out the memory, and answered Bren. 'I'll interview her myself...but she can wait in the outer office until I'm da— good and ready.'

Bren grinned and pretended to bow to him— which earned her a paper bird tossed in her hair. He often made origami when he was thinking up the dimensions of new inventions, needing to keep his hands busy while his mind worked.

His family were the only ones who could get away with any kind of irreverence with him. Everyone else was too afraid of his cool sarcasm. 'Heart of Ice' was his nickname in the press, and he was happy to keep it that way. It kept the nice women away from him—and fame-and-fortune-hunters deserved all they got—which was nothing but an occasional good time and their faces in the glossies.

'What's da—good, Unca Mark?' Shelby's big bright eyes were alight with curiosity.

He grinned down at his niece and pulled her ponytail, until she mock-shrieked and tugged hard at his nose. 'It means really, really good.'

'Okay,' Shelby replied, her face thoughtful. She knew he'd covered the truth and was trying to work out what he'd been about to say. She was a Hannaford, all right.

Bren got to her feet, rubbing her very pregnant belly. 'I'll tell Sylvie to wait. You'll pick me up tonight? Glenn felt so bad about asking, but since his trip is for Howlcat—'

He smiled, soft as he only ever was with his family, and handed Shelby to her mother. 'Can it, Bren. I can handle a couple of Lamaze classes as long as you introduce me as—'

His sister rolled her eyes. 'Yeah, yeah—as if calling you *George* is going to fool anyone when your face is in the papers every week.'

'Not every week,' he retorted mildly. He liked being called George every now and then. It made him smile.

She'd been waiting almost an hour.

Sylvie Browning smiled to herself. If he expected her to be put off or storm off he'd be disappointed. In the initial interview his sister

Brenda had warned her that meeting her prospec-
tive employer would be no picnic. Mark
Hannaford was hard-edged and cold, and he
didn't like his routine or privacy challenged—he
had no use for women, apart from the obvious.

That was why she was here. She had a fifteen-
year-old promise to keep.

After ninety minutes, the fanatically neat sec-
retary rose to her feet, and said, 'Mr Hannaford
will see you now.'

The older woman showed Sylvie in through
the massive oak double doors, opulent without
ostentation. 'Ms Browning to see you, sir.' Then
she closed the doors behind her.

Feeling the nervous grin stretching her face—
she always laughed or joked through stress, and
this was a tremendous moment—Sylvie walked
on low-polished floorboards and for a few
moments looked anywhere but at the CEO of
Howlcat Industries. There was a soft blue and
grey scatter rug on the floor. Pictures of the
harbour and the Blue Mountains lined the walls,
comfortable in their places.

What a lovely office, she thought to herself. It
suits—

'No. *No*.'

She blinked, and focussed on the sole occupant of the office. 'I beg your pardon?' she said softly, putting her hand out to him.

With the golden-brown hair and eyes, the lithe, athletic male body obvious even beneath the designer suit, she recognised him at once... But then, what Aussie *wouldn't* know him? He was one of the most famous men in the country. He hadn't inherited his empire, but pulled himself up by the bootstraps to this level of success by sheer brilliance. Inventor and lone wolf—tagged 'Heart of Ice' because no woman had ever come close to him.

Only his family—and she—knew better than that.

But at the moment he was living up to his reputation. He didn't stand to shake her hand, didn't touch her. His eyes were frozen as he said, with chilling clarity, 'I said, *no*. If you're Sylvia Browning, you are *not* being offered the position of housekeeper.'

Unfazed, she lifted her brows. This, too, she'd expected. She would change his attitude soon enough. She'd done it before, and she'd do it again. 'I know I look young, but I'm twenty-eight.'

Eyes filled with scepticism roamed her face. 'Twenty at the oldest. *No*.'

Since it was obvious he wasn't going to observe the most basic of social niceties, she dropped her hand and sat in the chair facing his desk. She rummaged in her handbag, pulled out her wallet and handed him the driver's licence and birth certificate from her CV packet.

He read them in silence, and handed them back without changing expression. 'Your age changes nothing, Ms Browning.'

'I was under the impression it changed *everything*.'

Her gently amused tone seemed to perturb him, for he frowned at her. 'Don't be impertinent.'

'I beg your pardon, Mr Hannaford,' she said gravely, but her telltale dimple quivered—she had only one, in her right cheek. Her brothers swore it gave her away when she was teasing. 'But, since you are *not* employing me, I'm free to be as impertinent as I like.'

His face stilled, then his mouth moved in a half-smile, slow as a rusted gate. '*Touché*, Ms Browning.'

Sylvie grinned at him, rose to her feet, and again put her hand out to his. 'It was nice meeting you, Mr Hannaford. I hope you find a house-keeper of the right age and appearance for you.' Her heart raced so fast she could barely keep up to breathe. Would it work?

He stood, too, but was still frowning. 'You're not going to try and convince me to give you the position?' he asked abruptly, again not taking her hand.

Her heart kicked up yet another notch—*yes*, there was the faintest tone of challenge there, as well as surprise. She made herself shrug. 'What's the point? I can cook and clean—but you don't care about that. I can make a home for you—but that isn't why you rejected me. I can only grow older in time, and I can't change the way I look.'

'There's nothing wrong with the way you look.'

His tone was still abrupt, but again something faint beneath it made her breath catch and her pulse move up a touch. 'Thank you,' she said as she turned towards the doors. 'I like to think I'm not totally repulsive.'

'You have to know you're a pretty woman.' But the comment was so far removed from a compli-ment—almost an insult in the hardness of his voice—that she didn't thank him.

'Are the curls natural?' he asked as he followed

her to the door—he was actually coming with her. She wanted to rejoice. Yes, she'd intrigued him.

'Yes, they are.' The answer was rueful. She touched the tumbling dark auburn curls escaping from her attempt at a chignon and looked up at him...really *up*. The top of her head barely reached his shoulder. 'Any attempt to straighten them only makes them frizz. Combine that with freckles, being only five-one and size eight, and I have to put up with everyone thinking I'm sixteen.'

She'd used the number deliberately, to see how he'd react. It was why she was here—why she'd come on this particular day—and she might as well start now.

His mouth tightened, but he only nodded. Then he frowned again, as if the number had triggered something inside him. 'Pardon me, Ms Browning, but I'm having the strangest sense of *déjà-vu*. Have we met?'

He'd remembered! She nodded, with a grin that felt silly on her face. He *remembered* her... 'For years I've wanted to thank you for all you did for my family. You'll never know what it meant to us—giving us the house, setting up the trust fund to send Simon to medical school, Joel to university, Drew to engineering college. When I found out this job was for *you*, it seemed a good chance to meet you again and thank you.'

For the first time he looked in her eyes, and she saw the change as he took in the face, the curls, and emotion dawned in him—recognition. 'Shirley Temple?' With his low growl, it was as if deep winter broke, giving way to a reluctant spring, and the warm-hearted boy she'd known when she was a girl peeked at her from beneath the frozen heart of the famous man.

'I go by Sylvie now.' For the third time she put her hand out, hoping he'd take it. She needed to know if the illusion she'd held for so many years would crumble under the force of reality—if she'd shrink or find him as terrifying as every other man she'd met since she turned fifteen.

'Sylvie?' His voice was deeper, rougher than she remembered it, but a warm shiver still ran through her. 'But your name's Mary Brown.'

'It's Mary Sylvia, actually, and we—the boys and I—liked Browning better. It was less common—especially for me, with a name like Mary.' Feeling embarrassed by the admission, she shrugged. 'I changed my name by deed poll, and the boys did the same.' She'd never tell him why she'd done it, or why the boys had followed her lead without hesitation. Although none of them had changed their first names, as well, as she had....

'Then Joel must have changed his only a few months ago.'

He knows how old we all are. He's kept up with us. The knowledge that he cared enough to know them, even from a physical and emotional distance, made her feel—feel—

Just *feel*. He hadn't forgotten her—as she'd never forgotten him.

Looking dazed, he put his hand in hers just as she was about to drop it. 'Look at you. You're all grown up.'

'So are you.' Her voice was breathless—but how could she help it? He was touching her again...and for the first time since she was fifteen a man's touch didn't repulse or terrify her. She felt warm and safe—and, given what her life had been, those feelings were as precious as gold to her.

From the first time she'd seen him at the hospital, when she'd been only eight, the prince of her fairytale dreams had changed from black-haired to dark blonde, from blue-eyed to golden-brown. Every time she'd met him after that, though months had passed, she'd felt the connection deepen, and when he'd held her in his arms and let her sleep the day her mother had died she'd known that, though it was the last day she'd see him for a very long time, no other boy would ever take his place.

Quiet lightning still strikes once—and never in the same spot. But he had lovers in abundance—all far more beautiful than she'd ever be—and they didn't come with her issues. Years ago she'd accepted that he was her impossible dream. That wasn't why she was here.

'So you really are twenty-eight?' He shook his head, as if trying to clear it.

'Yes.' As the juxtaposed longings to reach out and touch his face and to jerk her hand out of his and run all but overwhelmed her, she had to force her hand to stay where it was. Though she'd never been to counselling, she'd learned to conquer her fear to a manageable degree, by dint of the simple need to eat. If an employer thought she was crazy, he wouldn't employ her, and she couldn't always work with women.

His gaze swept her again. 'Your hair grew darker.'

'Red hair quite often does that.'

He was still holding her hand. Looking at his

expression as they touched, she sensed that it had been a long time since he'd truly touched anyone. 'Strawberry blonde.' He was smiling. 'You looked like a china doll.'

'According to some people I still do,' she said, sighing. 'Sometimes I'd give anything to be a few inches taller, if nothing else.'

'People don't take you seriously?' His voice held sympathy.

'You didn't,' she retorted, disliking the tone that seemed too close to pity, too close to how she'd been treated for so many years of her life. She pulled her hand from his.

'You're right.' He was looking at the broken connection, a strange expression in those frozen dreamer's eyes. 'Why do you want this position—or did you only come to thank me?'

His tone had lost the gentle warmth that made her glow. He wanted to be thanked even less than he'd appreciated her pointing out when he'd been in the wrong. By the look in his eyes, he also didn't want to hear any personal reasons for her answering his advertisement, on this of all days.

'I need the job,' she said abruptly. 'I'm in the final year of my nursing degree. I need somewhere to live and I need to pay the bills.'

'Why now?'

The simple question drew her out—the not-quite-cynical tone, the weary implication of *there must be a catch in this*. She stiffened her spine. It was all she could do not to walk out—but even her unconquerable pride was less important than keeping her word. But, oh, if she'd known it would be so hard to come back into his life this way, to stand before him and ask, she would never have made that promise to Chloe.

She heard the flat curtness in her voice as she finally answered. 'My flatmate Scott's getting married in a few weeks, and Sarah, his fiancée, wants to move her stuff in. I could live on campus, but I'd still need a job.'

'You still have the house?' It wasn't quite a question, more of an interrogation.

'Drew married his long-time girlfriend a while back—they had a baby boy five months after. They needed the house. He's in his third year of mechanical engineering, and with his study workload he can only work long enough hours to keep the family. Simon, Joel and I can get out there and pay rent.' She smiled at him, as if it was no big deal.

'I see.' And the tone, though restrained, told her he really did.

Mark looked down at the face of memory, an echo of sweetness long submerged. He saw in the pretty face of Sylvie Browning the girl she'd been. She didn't look as he'd expected except for her eyes—eyes still ancient in a young face—and her smile. The sweet, defiant smile of a girl who'd had to go to school while caring for her father and brothers, taking on a mother's role long before her mother had died.

Yes, he did understand her—too well. She'd accepted his money *for her family*. The one person he'd wanted to help through the years probably hadn't taken a cent for herself.

He shut himself off from the world with ice. Sylvie did it with a smile.

Behind the shutters he could make of his eyes, his famous brain raced. If she was desperate enough to play on a past so painful and intensely private, then she truly needed help—but she wouldn't accept his charity.

'Do you have references from past positions?'

As he'd judged, his cool detachment reassured her. Her shoulders relaxed and she breathed in deeply before she replied. 'Here's a reference from my boss at Dial-An-Angel, and some from many of my regular customers.'

She thrust a plastic sleeve at him, filled with letters.

His brows lifted as he read one glowing referral after another.

Honest, hard-working, discreet.

She made our house a home.

She became part of our family.

We offered her double to stay. We're so sorry to lose her.

'Impressive.' He noted she'd updated the references that stretched back a dozen years to fit her name change. She obviously wanted to leave her past behind for some reason—a reason he'd have to find out. He hadn't come this far in life by trusting anyone.

A wave of colour filled those soft-freckled cheeks. 'I didn't ask them to say it.'

The 'Heart of Ice' was famed for never descending to argument or reassurance on minor points. 'I have a contract all employees sign—including a confidentiality clause. If you sell a story or steal anything from me I'll sue you out of all human existence.'

She stared at him, and her flashing eyes—eyes the colour of old sherry, enormous, their curling lashes made thicker with mascara—held insult.

The colour grew in her face. Sweet indignation and adorable anger. Yet she was so much a woman at that moment the image of little brave Shirley Temple wavered and fell in his mind, shattering like glass on a tile floor.

'You'll sign it?' he pressed, fighting the ridiculous urge to take it back, to say he *knew* he could trust her. He hadn't seen her in fifteen years. He knew nothing about the woman apart from her stiff-necked refusal to accept help. That much about her hadn't changed a bit.

She nodded. 'I have one condition.'

He lifted a brow. None of his housekeepers had ever tried to bargain with him before; he made sure they didn't need to. 'Well?'

'I want to live in the cottage that comes with the job, but—' her eyes held the smiling defiance he'd seen in her as a girl, setting boundaries as well as he did, with all his cold control '—you don't come inside. *Ever.*'

He almost laughed in her face. What did she think? He hobnobbed with the help? He hadn't been in that place since he'd had it renovated years ago. 'Done. Now, please wait outside. If your references check out, the job's yours.'

'Thank you.' The words were cool, reserved,

but he felt *relief* inside. Oh, yeah, he understood that desperation and that pride, the need for personal space and dignity.

She walked out, her little feet in low-heeled sandals making no sound on his wooden flooring. He watched the sway of her gently flaring hips beneath the swishing skirt, saw the way her fists curled, her head held high, and didn't bother to call her former employers.

He was neither stupid nor blind. He knew inevitability when he saw it. Sylvie had the job, and she would live in the housekeeper's cottage behind his house for as long as she needed. If warning signs were flashing, if he felt as if he was standing in quicksand, he still couldn't do anything but hire her. If he let her down for the sake of his own security she'd haunt him for life: he'd be wondering where she was, what job she had, if they were good to her. He'd taken care of her by proxy for too many years to stop now.

Suddenly he wondered. *Did Bren know how he'd cared for the Brown family? Did she know it was Shirley Temple when she brought her here?*

Anger flooded his soul. Oh, yeah, Bren must have recognised Sylvie. By now the whole family must know that the child Sylvie had been made her the only woman who could break his defences on this day of all days. Why she'd come to him he didn't know, but he knew his family—still trying to rescue him from a life they abhorred, trying to break the ice around his heart. They were always trying to find him a woman like—

Didn't they know if he ever found another woman like Chloe he'd only run like hell? People like Chloe weren't meant to live long lives with guys like him. Just as Chloe had done, as little Mary had done, they touched your life and then left you—bereft, empty.

As empty as his heart and soul had become in the past fifteen years.

It was too late for redemption. None of his success changed what he'd done. No amount of money could take away the damage he'd inflicted on others—and Shirley Temple had come fifteen years too late.

Her name's Sylvie, and she's not a kid anymore, his mind taunted him. *Small, delicate, haunting, but she's a woman, head to foot.*

He clenched his fists, hating that just by telling him who she was she'd breached his defences. Her gentle face with its freckled prettiness was vulnerable and genuine, and it made him feel warm in a place he'd forgotten existed. But he couldn't let her get too close or she'd destroy him—and, worse, he'd destroy her.

He shuddered. *Never, never again.* No. It was time to erect a few barriers.

With cold deliberation he reached for the phone and, instead of calling Dial-An-Angel, he called a woman he'd dated once or twice—a model-actress as callous and uncaring as he'd been for years, who wanted only fun and a few minutes of fame.

If Sylvie was in the cottage behind his waterfront mansion tonight, she'd be alone. He'd be out on the town with Toni, doing what he did best: forgetting there had ever been someone who loved him just as he was, and who pushed him to be his best.

On this day he had two choices: drink, or take a woman to a hotel.

As usual, he chose the latter.

Balmain

Sylvie wandered through the house, wide-eyed, whispering, 'Oh,' every few moments. Built in 1849 by a ship's captain, right on Sydney Harbour, Mark's house was a fascinating waterfront blend of colonial, naval and Victorian, with open beams, leadlight windows and wide-planked flooring; the outside was sandstone blocks.

It was a dream come true—the kind of dream she'd have had if she'd known this wonderful, eclectic, *homey* house existed. It was almost perfect...*almost*.

She grinned. So he had a date tonight? So what? Because of him, she now had a home, and a job that would pay the bills and allow her to save while she finished college. She was so deeply in his debt she doubted she'd ever be able to climb out—and she'd promised Chloe she'd take care of him. It was time for her to do some giving...and she knew where to start: the Friday night markets at The Rocks.

By running all the way to the ferry stop on the harbour, she just made the next ferry.

CHAPTER TWO

Later that night

MARK had to hold back from slamming the door.

What was wrong with him?

After the Lamaze classes, where he hadn't missed a single opportunity to get the message across to Bren, he'd dropped her home and taken Toni, a stunning woman, for a late dinner and dancing at the best clubs. And he'd made sure his sister knew where he was going.

He'd fulfilled his part, given Toni the exposure she needed. She was currently between jobs, and being photographed with him would make all the tabloids. It was a guarantee that producers and casting agencies would remember to call her. In return, she'd have been happy to spend the rest of the night with him at a hotel—she didn't want the intimacy of spending the night at her place or his, either—and yet he'd still said, 'Another time…'

Toni's amused acceptance of his being so able to keep his hands off her perfect tanned body hadn't helped things, either. 'So, what's her name?'

He'd had a ridiculous urge to snap back, *Shirley Temple.*

And it was the truth. Oh, not sexually—it was guilt. After she'd signed the contract, he'd tossed his spare keys at a bemused Sylvie, scrawled the address on a piece of paper for her, and told her the housekeeper's cottage was out at the back and to move in over the weekend. He'd said he expected breakfast at six twenty-five Monday morning, and he wouldn't be home tonight.

All she'd said was, 'Of course. Thank you for everything.'

Her good manners in the face of his rudeness had made him all the more appalled that he'd lost his manners with the wrong person. She'd come to thank him—to answer a job advertisement. He'd taken out his anger with Bren on Sylvie.

He owed her an apology, and he didn't like its effect on him. She'd stayed on his mind, haunting him with her brave, defiant smile and her acceptance of his bad temper, until he hadn't even felt Toni when she'd kissed him.

So now he was home alone, thinking of *his housekeeper* when he could have been naked with a gorgeous blonde, forgetting the past for an hour. And now he probably wouldn't sleep because he felt totally screwed up, screwed over, angry and *ashamed*. And Sylvie was bound to be sleeping so he couldn't offload his conscience until morning—

And then every thought vanished.

He flicked on the lights and stood in the middle of the entryway, breathing. What was that amazing smell? Inhaling again, he felt the turbulence inside his soul vanish, leaving only traces of its memory behind. He felt uplifted, energised, *inventive*…

The house was different, too—wasn't it?

He went into one room after another, flicking on lights. He'd never seen that stained-glass sailing ship on the living room wall before, or that chart beside the entry to the ballroom—a print of Captain Cook's pencilled route to Botany Bay. Funny, he had to look at them twice to notice, but now he looked there seemed to be little changes everywhere.

Even the lights weren't the same—the lights

themselves were softer, lending a gentle night radiance to every room it hadn't had before.

What had Sylvie done to his house?

Breathing in the amazing scent, he wandered from room to room, seeing the touches so sweet and subtle he still had to look twice to find them. It was as if they'd grown here while he'd been gone. A funny little scarecrow doll sat proudly on his kitchen windowsill, bearing the legend 'Housework Makes You Ugly'. A plain grey river stone sat on his study desk in front of his monitor, with a single word on it: *Believe*. Two of his stupid origami pieces sat either side of the stone, as if to say *Your creations*.

Dried herbs hung from the edges of curtains. There was a bright flowered tablecloth on his grandma's dining table, a vase filled with purple flowers from his garden. Tiny pictures hung on the kitchen walls, old soap and butterscotch ads in wooden frames. A distressed wooden hanging was on the dining room wall, proudly bearing a kookaburra in military get-up, proclaiming the efficacy of Diggaburra Tea. Another faced it, this time a teddy bear saluting him, telling him to drink Teddy Beer.

Everything was scrupulously clean, polished,

but it looked… He didn't know—but after his fury of a minute before, now all he wanted was to smile. The glowing floors, the scent, the additions to his furniture made him want to laugh. Stupid clutter to him—he'd *never* have bought it himself—yet somehow it announced her presence in his life. *I'm here, Mark.*

She knew how to make an impact.

It was just so—so *Sylvie*, he thought grimly, trying to muster up some negative emotion and failing. Confused by all the foreign emotion churning in him—he was feeling *happy* when he should be mad—he stalked to the back door, jerked it open and shouted in the general direction of the cottage, 'Sylvie!'

He refused to repeat himself. He'd yelled loud enough the first time.

Moments later a light came on in the cottage, then the door opened and a sleepy voice said softly, 'I think knocking would be kinder to the neighbours at this time of night.'

He cursed beneath his breath. 'Could you come inside, please?' he asked, in as reasonable a manner as possible.

'Answering to the boss at 2:47 a.m. wasn't in the contract…sir.'

She was right. He was caught in the wrong again—and the fact only made him want to fight more. 'Tomorrow at six.'

'Technically, it's today, sir—and it's a Saturday. Do I have weekends off?'

The word *sir* got him all fidgety. It wasn't right coming from her, after their shared past, and he suspected she only did it now to make a point. 'Just come inside *now*!'

He heard a distinct sigh, but a figure emerged from the warm darkness.

Mark caught his breath. Tumbled curls, mussed with sleep, fell around her shoulders, catching the light until they looked like dark fire. Her face was rosy, her eyes big, cloudy—and she was wearing a slip nightie in a soft clear blue that showcased her pale skin like pearls in shimmering water.

She stood outside the door, dropped some slippers to the mat, and shoved her feet into them. She sent him an enquiring glance. 'You did want me to come in now?' she asked, nodding at the door he still held.

'What? Oh, yes.' He moved back and she walked into the kitchen, throwing a cotton robe over her nightie.

He nearly growled in protest. She'd looked so

sweet and silky, so touchable with her bare feet, and her body—the curves were small, but in the iridescent half-light she'd looked like a creature of magic and moonlight.

She rubbed her eyes and blinked. 'Is this kind of awakening going to be a regular occurrence, sir? If so, I'll have to go to bed earlier.'

'Stop calling me *sir*,' he snapped.

Sylvie sighed again. 'Mr Hannaford is such a mouthful…but whatever you wish.'

'I've already warned you about impertinence. I won't tolerate it.'

She frowned and tilted her head. 'I'm sorry, but I'm not at my best this time of night. Are you saying that calling you Mr Hannaford is impertinent?'

'I'm saying—' He shook his head. How had they descended to this level so fast? And how could he have fallen in lust so fast with someone he'd thought of as Shirley Temple? Until he'd seen her like this, as if she'd come fresh from a lover's bed. 'I don't argue with employees.'

She smiled at him, a sleepy thing of flushed beauty that made him catch his breath and his body harden with an urgency all Toni's kisses hadn't been able to rouse. 'You can't imagine how glad I am to hear that—given our…um…conversation of the past few minutes. So, to sort matters, what *would* you like me to call you?'

Locked into the unexpected desire that had hit him with the force of a ten-pound grenade, he said huskily, 'Mark will do.'

The way that single crinkle between her brows grew told him what she thought of *that*. 'I thought you wanted some professional distance between us?'

He shrugged, trying not to laugh. Oh, she knew how to call him on his pronouncements, and she wasn't a bit intimidated by anything he did or said. 'Distance seems fairly silly at the moment, given where we are and what you're wearing—and our shared past.'

With an endearing self-consciousness she pulled her robe around her. 'I'd feel better if you smiled.' Her eyes were big as she stared at him with haunting uncertainty. China-doll lovely, and so tempting…

'Please, Sylvie, call me Mark,' he murmured—and smiled.

She swallowed and moistened her lips, her eyes still huge, unsure. 'Thank you—Mark.'

A little half-smile lingered on her mouth. She always smiled—unless her prickly pride was touched. She seemed to have hidden laughter lurking around her, a delicious mirth he thought she might share with him if he got close enough. He took a step forward, obeying the imperative urge to imbibe her sparkling warmth, to touch—

Sylvie caught the back of her slipper on a mat as she took a hasty step back.

And he remembered at the worst possible moment what he was doing, where this was going. She was his employee, in a vulnerable position—and, much as he wanted to forget it, she *was* Shirley Temple. Her memory shone in his mind like starlight: for five years she'd been the girl who'd given him silent empathy when no one else had understood he didn't *want* to talk, who'd been there for him when he'd felt lost and alone, cared for him when she'd had no one to care for her. She'd simply given him what he'd needed when he'd needed it, in a no cost or agenda way.

She was still doing it now—giving without taking back—and while his craving body was reminding him that she was most definitely a woman, she was only here because he'd ordered her inside. Hours after duty ended.

Her duties haven't even begun yet, jerk. She's barely had time to move her stuff in.

She'd suffered enough in her life, if the report he'd received this afternoon was true. She didn't know the shallow games he played with women; she'd been too busy caring for her father until his death, bringing up her brothers. She'd only begun to have a life of her own when Joel had moved into the dorm rooms at his university. *Three months ago.*

His hands curled into fists of denial. He couldn't be the hard-hearted man on the town. No matter how much he wanted to forget what this day was, he couldn't do it to her.

'So…what did you want to talk about?' she asked, the breathless sound in her voice sweet and pretty.

Everything about Sylvie was pretty—from her tousled curls to her pink-painted toes peeping out from the open-ended slippers. And so were the changes she'd made to his house.

His anger seemed ridiculous now. 'I owe you an apology for my rudeness at the office.'

She yawned behind her hand with a puzzled look. 'You yelled the street down at 2:47 a.m. to apologise?'

He felt heat creeping up his neck.

Her grin was as sweet as the look in her eyes—

a mixture of woman and imp. 'I was sure you were going to bawl me out for the presents I brought you.'

'Why did you do it?' he asked abruptly.

She shuffled her slippers on the floor, staring at her feet. 'Every good thing in my life has come from you.' She shrugged with one shoulder, her neck tilting to meet its uplift, and he knew what she was about to say. 'It isn't in me to do nothing but take, Mark. I know there's nothing I can give you to thank you for rescuing my family—but I wanted to try.'

Any lingering anger, any urge to bawl her out or freeze her out, withered and died under the pure, humbling honesty of her. 'Anything I ever gave you can never repay what you did for me.'

She looked up again, her smile shy and eager, and though he saw an echo of the Shirley Temple he remembered, she was a rosy, tumbled woman at the same time. She was both and more—and she fascinated him too much for her own good. He had to get her to stay away from him, because he wasn't having any success in staying away from her.

'When the deed for the house came, and the trust for us, and the card from you… You have no idea what you did for me—us.'

Her words, sincere and choked with emotion, annihilated his normal method of making a woman keep her distance. 'You, Sylvie,' he said quietly, wondering why he said it. 'I did it for *you*.'

'You saved my life.' She looked at him as if he was wonderful. 'Literally, you saved me, Mark. When the money came I was drowning. Dad was too sick to work, I was working part-time at a restaurant to make the rent, going to school, cleaning houses, doing homework at midnight. I—' She swallowed, and then said abruptly, 'Owning the house helped me put food on the table, paid for a housekeeper. I could stay at school, study and pass my exams.'

'It was just money.' He wanted to turn away, but he couldn't stand not to see her flushed prettiness, the shining gratitude and hidden pain in those lovely eyes.

'No.' She took a step towards him, tender, hesitant. 'Your house is so beautiful. I can feel your love for it in all the old furniture. I love it, too. It's like you.'

Too many emotions crowded him; he hadn't felt this confused since he was about thirteen, and her last comment heightened his bemusement. 'Like me?'

She nodded, her face serious. 'I walked in this afternoon and felt as if it was a haven in a crazy city. I felt peace. You could have made this a showplace. Instead you chose furniture that made it mellow, gentle and welcoming. It's a family house for a family man.'

Alarm bells shrieked in his head. *Don't do it. Don't lose it with her.* And still he stepped forward, looking over her—such a delicate woman—and snarled in a freezing tone, 'Do you *see* a family here?' She jerked back fast, breathing unevenly, her face white, and with such terror in her eyes he felt horrified. 'Sylvie, I didn't mean to—'

She lifted a shaking hand and he stopped. Just like that. He who hadn't obeyed any woman but his mother for over a decade. Was it their past, or the shimmering tears in her eyes that halted him before her?

When she spoke it was in a half-whisper, with the shadows of her fear hovering around her like an aura of night. 'I see the ghosts of the family that *should* be here. This house is the real you…it's your haven from being the Heart of Ice. You bought this house for *her*. For Chloe, for both of you—it's everything you should have had with her. The family, the babies.'

He felt the blood drain from his head, leaving him dizzy. By God, she met a sword-thrust with gentle atom bombs—and he couldn't take any more reminders of what he'd become, what he'd always be now: a man alone.

'Go to bed, Sylvie. Have the weekend off to settle into the cottage. Don't worry about my breakfast. Just don't come in here until I'm gone.' The words grated like sandpaper in his throat.

'All right.' She turned and walked to the door, not wishing him a goodnight. Probably she knew it wasn't, and it wouldn't be. All he wanted now was for her to leave him alone. All he wanted was to drown himself in Scotch. If only he had any of the stuff in the house.

An echo rang in his heart and head—an anthem of unending loss. Not of Chloe herself—he'd accepted that a year before her death—but loss of hope. He'd lost something vital inside himself long before her death, and he'd never found it again.

At the door, Sylvie spoke again. 'Mark?'

He gripped a dining chair, knowing that whatever she was about to say would be unexpected. She wasn't fooled by his cover. She didn't see him as the Heart of Ice, wasn't intimidated by his anger, wasn't over-awed by his power or wealth. She saw *Mark*. She knew what he'd once been—believed that boy was still inside him somewhere—and that scared the living daylights out of him. He couldn't be that person again. He couldn't open his heart to any woman. Even Sylvie.

Especially Sylvie. She was everything he'd avoided for fifteen years—the kind of woman who'd take what was left of his heart and soul and rip it to shreds.

'What?' He closed his eyes, waiting for the blow. He already knew she had that power.

When she spoke, he heard the shaking in her voice as strongly as he felt the trembling in his limbs. 'Chloe deserves you to have bought this house for her. She deserves to be remembered and to be loved still. And you deserve this refuge. Time out from the cold and uncaring person you never were inside.'

He hung on to the chair like grim death as pain raced through his body and soul like a heat blast, leaving him scalded and weak. *She doesn't know the truth. Don't tell her. Don't say it!*

'Just go. *Please*.' The words came out in a strangled voice.

The door closed behind her, and he was left

alone with the endless ghost of grief, guilt and regret. All he wanted now was to talk to a friend in a black-labelled bottle.

He'd been wishing that for the past fifteen years. All he could drown himself in now was meaningless sex…and it never helped him forget who he was. *What* he was.

Sylvie closed the door of her new home, closed her eyes and gulped in shaking breaths.

She should never have said it. The agony in his eyes had told the truth about the infamous Heart of Ice. He wrapped himself inside a coldness that could shatter at a touch. But it was nothing but a delicate veneer, hiding his private emotions from a world that didn't want to see, didn't want to know the man beneath the legend.

So *stupid*! She'd known it was too early.

If he snarled at her like that again he wouldn't have to fire her; she'd run like the frightened jackrabbit she was—even though she *knew* he'd never hurt her.

Leaning against the door, because she didn't think her legs would carry her further, she kept trying to breathe while her ears strained for the sound of his footsteps. She was pulling herself together, ready to smile in the face of disaster. Waiting and waiting.

Only the soft lapping of waves behind her cottage greeted her.

He wasn't coming. Of course he wasn't— because he was Mark and she was Shirley Temple, the girl who'd handed him a wet flannel, a few glasses of water, given him some hugs and held his hand. And yet he'd treasured what little she'd done for him enough to seek the family out and save them when she'd reached desperate measures to pay the rent and put food on the table, with threats of Welfare stepping in to take the boys away.

From the moment Brenda had recognised her at the job interview today, her words had cemented what Sylvie had long suspected. Mark's family loved him but didn't understand him. They wanted to *push* him into happiness so they could stop worrying about him. It was love, but not the love he needed.

Just like her brother Simon, who tried to match her up with men all the time: men who were gentle, who wouldn't rush her. Men who might as well have been invisible for all she could feel for them.

'Stop reaching for the stars,' Simon always said. 'You'll never see him again.'

But she'd rather live her life alone than with any man who wasn't the one. Mark had been her childhood prince, but he might have faded from her memory if he hadn't saved her life, saved her family…saved her from the unbearable choice facing her when the money came. And the prince of her little-girl fantasies had become her teenage hero. Then finally, when she'd seen the tabloid stories on him, seen the frozen suffering beneath the wolfish smile, he'd become her love, so entwined in her heart she'd never leave him behind.

The Heart of Ice wasn't the boy she remembered, who'd stood beside a dying girl for years, even marrying her rather than running when it all became too hard. The boy who'd felt sick at the thought of giving a promise to love another girl because it would be a lie. Maybe all he wanted was to be left in peace with his memories but she'd given a promise, made sacred by death. At the right time she'd given up her home, her job security—and most importantly, her secure anonymity—to come to Mark and keep her vow.

Though she had nothing to speak of, she had something she could give Mark that he didn't have: a true home, a *friend*... And if she could pull off a miracle, maybe she could help him learn to live again.

CHAPTER THREE

SYLVIE was in the kitchen Monday morning, making breakfast while Mark was out running, when the phone rang. She checked the oven clock: six-fourteen. She was sure Mark carried a mobile phone and a pager. She shouldn't take his private calls. But by the fourth time it started ringing she'd realised the caller knew Mark was out. She picked up.

'So, how's it going, Sylvie?' Brenda's eager voice came the second she said hello.

'Fine,' she said warily. How would you describe a weekend where your employer had seemed to work all hours while you moved non-existent furniture around, aching to move your feet thirty metres but you'd been banned until Monday? And how did you say that to your employer's sister whom you barely knew— hadn't seen in fifteen years?

'So, how's Mark? Is he talking to you? Has he said anything?'

She bit her lip. This was her first real day of work. The course of wisdom was telling her to take her time—but, being Bigmouth Sylvie, she did the opposite. 'Brenda, I appreciate you helped me get the job, but whatever Mark says to me remains between us. End of subject. I need this job, and I'm not about to risk it by being unprofessional—'

'Sylvie, Mark needs you,' Brenda said bluntly. 'You've seen how he is. He's not our Mark—the boy you knew.'

Sylvie sighed. 'You can't throw women at Mark like mud and hope one sticks. You can't heal him; he can only do that himself. And calling me for updates is something I never agreed to. I'm only here to cook and clean.' She almost added, *For all you know, I could be romantically involved,* but she remembered Brenda's specific questions on her romantic status, with the excuse that Mark would welcome no overnight guests. 'I haven't seen him in fifteen years, but I'm sure of one thing: your anxiety probably makes him feel bad that he can't make you feel better—and that makes it worse for him.'

Silence greeted her declaration for a few moments. 'I'm sorry.' Brenda's voice had gone stiff and cold. 'Wouldn't you be anxious about your brother if he was like Mark?'

Before Sylvie could answer, the bleeping sound of disconnection filled her ear. She sighed and hung up, turning back to the breakfast she was making.

'Thank you.'

She whirled around. Wearing exercise gear that moulded to his body like a second skin, he stood in the open doorway between the kitchen and dining room, hot and sweaty from his run, his dark-blond hair plastered to his skull. He was still breathing heavily.

'You're welcome.' Her throat was thick, her heart pounding so hard it was as if she'd been running with him. Shocked by the depth of her response to him, she whirled to face the oven. She'd never felt desire in her life before, but the aching of her body, the itching in her fingertips to touch him, couldn't be anything else. 'I know I crossed the line, but she kept calling. She said…' Hot colour scorched her face. She was talking about his *sister*!

'I knew she would. Persistence and interference

are the Hannaford middle names.' He spoke with loving resignation. 'The only mystery is why the other girls haven't called or come over yet—you remember my sisters Becky and Katie—or my mother. You ought to expect them, though. Beware: they'll dig and dig until they get what they want,' he said, sounding surprised he'd said anything so personal.

To cut off the coldness she sensed was coming—his way of trying to keep a professional distance—she spoke in a flat tone. 'I'll be at college.' She opened the oven door. 'I hope coming in early to make breakfast is acceptable?'

'For something that smells like that, you can come in before dawn.' He breathed in deeply. 'That smells incredible. What is it?'

Trying to hide a grin of delight—Brenda had told her that he preferred health foods—she said neutrally, 'Just some home-baked muesli and fresh coffee.'

'Home-baked? I don't think *that* was in the contract.' But the way he inhaled, the smile as he did so, told her he wasn't about to argue. 'I usually eat fruit.'

'I made fruit salad, too.' She turned back to the food before he could comment, unsure whether he would say something kind or would freeze her. 'It'll be ready when you are.'

Fifteen minutes later he was wolfing down breakfast as she cleaned. 'That was superb,' he said as he brought the bowls and cup to her. 'Thank you, Sylvie.'

'You're welcome.'

Strange how such polite words and praise could hide so much. Somewhere between his coming in on her conversation with Brenda and his return from the shower he'd remembered her interference on Friday night. The air was strained, the tension almost visible; it would only become worse if she apologised. All they were leaving unsaid hovered in the air between them like a comic dialogue balloon—you could choose not to read it but it was still *there*.

He said a curt goodbye as he was leaving—before seven.

'I'll have dinner waiting,' she said, not knowing why she'd said it or what she was hoping for.

His cold reply was all she deserved for poking her nose in again. 'I'm rarely home before nine.'

He worked fourteen-hour days on a regular basis? 'I'll have it ready for eight, in case.'

She cursed her clumsy mouth—setting rules in

his home. She didn't expect an answer, and didn't get one.

When he roared out of the garage she shrugged, ate her share of breakfast, put on her cleaning music, ran through the house until it was sparkling, and left for college before the family he'd forewarned her about could arrive.

'So how's the new housekeeper?' his brother Pete asked after the morning meeting was done, and he, Pete and Glenn, his brother-in-law, were alone.

'Tell Bren if she wants an update to ask me herself.'

Glenn chuckled, and Pete grinned. 'The Heart of Ice stuff doesn't work on me, bro. I've shared a room with you, punched you up, stood beside you when the football jocks attacked us, and covered up for you when you and Chloe did midnight flits to invent something.'

Glenn laughed again, and agreed.

Mark smiled reluctantly. They'd all been close from school days. Pete, only a year younger than him, was his Chief IT Officer, and Glenn, besides being Bren's husband, was Financial Controller for Howlcat. Nerds United, they used to call themselves; but they'd stuck together through good times and bad, and there were no two men he trusted more.

'So, how is she? You know Mum's sure to call me and ask.'

Mark gave an exaggerated sigh. 'We fell in love at first sight, made passionate love all night and we are eloping on our first day off. *Now* will you get off my back?'

Pete's brows lifted. 'I only meant to ask if she can cook and clean all right, since I know you did her a favour in hiring her,' he said mildly.

Mark found himself flushing. 'She makes muesli to die for, keeps the house in perfect order.' He tried to stop himself, but the stress in him had been building like a pressure cooker on high all weekend, and it had to come out. 'She also says everything she shouldn't, gives me presents that make my house hers somehow, then says something so *sweet* I can't tell her off. She doesn't act like any employee I've known, but I can't fire her because—' The words burst from him. 'She's Shirley Temple—all right? Remember the kid whose dying mother was in the hospice the same time as Chloe a lot? She's been through hell since then, and she deserves a break.'

His brother and his friend both nodded, but there was a suspicious twinkle in both sets of eyes, and he knew what was coming. 'I saw her the other day. She's a real cutie,' Glenn said.

'Adorable, if you like the type,' Pete added, grinning. 'Pretty and sweet. Just as well you prefer sophisticated women to china dolls.'

He was lying, and they all knew it. He growled in agreement and stalked out of the conference room to his haven in Howlcat Industries, pulling off his jacket and tie on the way. Nobody bothered him in the basement lab except in an emergency—even his mother.

Why he was home by seven-thirty he didn't know. She was his *housekeeper*, he wasn't accountable to her—but the good manners his mother had instilled in him came into play. If dinner was ready by eight, he'd be there.

Though he was still angry at her less-than-subtle manipulation of his working day, after the breakfast she'd made this morning his stomach was reminding him he didn't have to get takeout, heat a frozen meal or eat at his parents' tonight and answer the inevitable questions.

He came in the back way, and his reward for

leaving work was immediate. The smell from the oven made his mouth water and his stomach growl double-time. Baking garlic, cheese and pasta…and music wafted from his ballroom.

He walked as far as the entryway and saw a fairy sprite tripping across the floorboards.

Literally.

She was barefoot, wearing cut-off denim shorts and a lavender tank top, her hair in a ponytail, with dark red spirals falling around her face and shoulders. Her arms were stiffly held out to an invisible partner, her face serious, her kissable mouth pursed as she dipped her head with each first movement. '*One*, two, three…*one*, two, three…'

And she tripped sideways, stumbled and recovered with a sigh.

Adorable Sylvie might be—graceful she was not.

He halted three times on his way, before he threw caution to the winds for the first time in years, crossed the room and moved into her arms. 'Straighten your back.'

She gasped and fell against him—but, ignoring his body's reaction to her gentle curves, to the soft scent of her skin, he pulled her up and held her with the right distance and strength.

'Your posture's off, which is why you keep tripping, Sylvie. Now, straighten up and follow my lead.'

She blinked, and blinked again, gulping and wetting her mouth. Her face was filled with a mixture of wonder and trepidation, and something lurking beneath he couldn't identify. 'You—you can dance?'

He nodded, intrigued. Yeah, Glenn had it right: she *was* cute, but something he couldn't work out caught and held him. 'Three years of lessons, on and off.' Chloe had nagged him into it the year before her cancer diagnosis. 'Now—*posture.*'

After a hesitation so palpable he thought she was going to walk away, she stood as tall as her delicate frame would allow. She was stiff in his arms, her gaze focusing straight ahead on nothing, as if he wasn't there. Or she didn't *want* him to be there.

'What's next?'

The two brusque words didn't invite questions. 'Feet facing mine, five inches apart.'

She checked her feet in evident anxiety, then looked back at him with the same anxiety quickly masked.

'Look up at me. I'll tell you when it's right.'

Big mistake. She looked in his eyes, hers earnest and apprehensive all at once—and she was *blushing*. He almost forgot what he was doing.

'Is this right?'

Her voice was breathless, the heat in her cheeks filling her throat, and the alarm bells in his head were shrieking. She'd either danced herself into high blood pressure, was terrified of him—or his touch was affecting her as much as hers did him.

'It's right.' He almost croaked, but controlled it with a strong effort. When he touched other women the silky-softness he felt was bought with expensive lotions in stores. Sylvie was a slip of moonlight in his arms, and the satin of her skin was as natural as the simple clothing she wore. 'Now, follow. Your count was right, but it's hard to dance the woman's part without a lead.'

Without a word she followed him when he stepped forward.

Now she moved well. In following him she lost her endearing clumsiness, became graceful—and the situation lifted to high alert without her even trying to flirt with him.

Why had he forgotten the rule? *Never touch the kind of woman he liked best.* That way led to madness and loss, the road to fury, drinking, regrets—and rehab. He never wanted to repeat *that* time. So he played with women who wouldn't expect more than his money could give. He couldn't get over his loss, find someone new and move on. He felt too much, hurt too much. Fell apart when—

'*One*, two, three…*one*, two, three…'

So serious, concentrating on each step. The tip of her tongue popped out between counts as she thought about her feet. He didn't tell her she didn't have to think beyond her posture now. A good male lead could keep his partner in step in most social situations—and he was guessing Sylvie wasn't practising for a contest or celebrity show.

'This is for the wedding, right?' he guessed.

She nodded, looking flustered still, a little scared—and so kissable it was all he could do to hold back. 'I'm maid of honour. Sarah wants a real waltz for her bridal dance. She and Scott have been taking lessons for two months.' Her voice held a wealth of love and a multitude of dark secrets—and he didn't have to ask why she hadn't paid for lessons.

A *ping* sound floated in from the kitchen.

'Dinner's ready.' She stood staring at him, the blush growing by the moment—as was his urgency.

For years sex had been a physical release on days when he needed to forget the pain—occasionally urgent when it had been months since he'd bothered with a woman. Now the urgency was hitting him like a king tide...but this was *Sylvie*. He didn't deserve a woman as luminous and pure as her—and she sure as hell didn't deserve the screw-up beneath his wealth and fame.

'Please let me go.'

It was only then he realised he'd been holding her so tight she couldn't break out of his arms without struggling. Feeling like a fool, he dropped his hands. 'Smells delicious. I'm hungry. What is it?'

She'd already stepped out of his dance zone—out of his zone altogether. She did the one-shoulder shrug thing again, looking at the floor. 'Just vegetable lasagne and some garlic bread. Nothing special.'

'If it's anything like the home-baked muesli this morning, I'll be home for dinner any night you make it,' he said, wondering why she always demeaned her skills.

The colour intensified in her cheeks, and he wanted to hit himself. 'I didn't mean to make you feel compelled to cook for me every night, Sylvie.'

Another half-shrug, defensive, keeping him at a distance. 'It's what I do.'

He remembered the references he'd read about offering her double to stay, making a house a home, and he no longer felt special or flattered that she was going out of her way for him.

What a jerk, imagining more, based on lustful hopes and her blush, which could so easily be simple embarrassment at the boss touching her.

Since he couldn't avoid her, it seemed there was only one way to get through this: cauterisation. He'd have to touch her and touch her until he felt nothing.

'How about a deal?' He made his voice casual as he led the way into the kitchen. 'Your food is so wonderful it makes me feel like I owe you. You need to learn the waltz. I know how. So, you cook for me and I'll teach you to dance.'

He took two dinner plates from the cupboard without thinking about it, and handed them to her. After a second's hesitation she put them down and began ladling food onto one, then the other, and took two sets of cutlery from the drawer. She didn't answer him about the dancing, and he didn't push the offer.

Strangely delighted by her tacit acceptance—that she wasn't making more of a simple sharing of a meal than it was—he got out a bottle of chianti from his wine rack and lifted it in silent query, wondering if she'd notice that, though it was imported from Italy, it was non-alcoholic. A permanent reminder that he'd never be normal again.

She nodded and smiled at him, her face all rosy again, and though it could easily be the oven's heat, she looked so lovable....

No! She was *likable*, that was it. Not *love*. Never love.

But it was funny how they communicated so well without words.

And, for no reason he could fathom, cold fear gripped his soul. He *wanted* to spend time with Sylvie, talking or silent, and yet only three days ago he'd felt nearly sick with relief when she'd left him alone. Things had changed so fast he couldn't get a handle on it—on what was happening or why he wanted her company.

What did it matter? When she wasn't with him he thought of her anyway, and it would be a terrible lapse in manners to withdraw the unspoken invitation. He might as well have the pleasure of looking at her.

As he cut off his first mouthful of lasagne, he asked, 'So, how was college? You said you're doing nursing?'

She nodded, smiling. 'I think it was inevitable—that or a kindergarten teacher. I like looking after people.'

'You do it well.' A burst of flavour exploded in his mouth and he groaned. 'This is marvellous. Did you ever think of becoming a chef?'

She shook her head. 'I love to cook. It's fun for me. If I had to do it for a living it wouldn't be fun anymore.'

'I still love inventing.' In fact, during his sojourn in the basement today he'd come up with a new use for the original Howlcat patent: a way to reduce engine noise pollution in planes on takeoff and landing if he could find the right materials for the application.

'Of course you do. What's not to like?' She grinned, and he began to relax. Whatever was bothering her, she was finally letting go—at least for now. 'In charge of your company, able to tell people to hike off when you're thinking, making millions every time you say, "I've got an idea...."'

'It's not quite that simple.' He laughed.

'It can't be if you're the boss and you still have to work thirteen, fourteen hours a day.'

'Well, I do have to actually make the things— you know, gather materials, work engines, make it work in practice, as well as on paper.'

Her eyes twinkled. 'You mean you have to *work* for those millions?' she asked in mock-horror. 'And here I thought you spent all day playing the part of famous playboy.'

He didn't answer that. In his opinion, being a playboy was one of the best and worst parts all at once—because though he had fun it was still, as she'd so beautifully put it, *playing the part*; it wasn't Mark. 'There are some downsides to the life.'

She sobered immediately. 'I'm sorry. My sense of humour sometimes takes me to strange and exotic places. Simon always says it'll be the death of me.'

Sylvie said the words with light deliberation, smiling in the hope that he would accept the words without going too deep.

'Death by laughter? An appropriately Sylvie thing to happen—and typical of me that I'd hire you. I'm sure there's a hint of the masochist in me somewhere.'

Relieved far more than she'd show that he hadn't overreacted to her death comment and asked her to leave, she lifted her wineglass and saluted him. 'To men who make a living by howling cats, and women who want to laugh themselves into oblivion.'

He touched his glass to hers. 'That's just a goofball way of saying "To us".' But he was chuckling, and she joined in, hiding the tightening of her chest at the mere thought of there ever being an 'us' for them.

She had to get over this ridiculous infatuation! So stupid to dream when she *knew* there could be nothing. He'd seen her reaction to his touch; he knew something was wrong with her. She *had* to get over him. She had no choice, because she knew three things with all her soul: she was nothing like the beautiful, sophisticated women he dated now; she could never live up to Chloe in either his eyes or her own—and she'd never be a normal woman.

'So, you think you know me after a few days?' she challenged him after they'd eaten in silence for a minute or two.

He shrugged. 'Expect the unexpected is your motto, I suspect.'

Her mouth twitched in acknowledgement, but she said, 'I knew what to expect for too long. Now the boys are settled and happy, Dad died peacefully at home, and I want to rejoice in every day—to celebrate life, always looking forward.'

And never look back to what I was—what I had to do to survive.

Instead of seeing the message for him in her words—why could she never shut up and enjoy his company without trying to heal him?—Mark leaned forward, his hand almost touching hers. She jerked back before she could stop herself, and though his gaze followed the movement, he didn't comment on it.

'After all you've been through you deserve to celebrate life, to be happy. I hope you find reasons to celebrate each day.'

She frowned, tilting her head as the implications of his words sank in, going far deeper than the little she'd told him. 'You had me investigated?'

His gaze was dark, hooded. 'I have everyone I employ investigated, Sylvie. I have to.'

But why me? she wanted to yell at him. *Surely you trust me?*

A thought as insidious as poison crept into her

soul. *What does he know? What else did he find out?*

But he couldn't know. Though her younger brothers and Scott suspected something had happened to her, nobody knew but Simon and Mr Landsedge. If he ever decided to tell—

He won't unless it becomes worth his while— such as if I became involved with a rich, famous man. And that was why fulfilling any part of her promise to Chloe was fraught with danger. Yet here she was…

'I'm amazed you didn't do it years ago—before you sent the money,' she bit out.

He stiffened, didn't speak for long, uncomfortable moments, and she almost squirmed, waiting for what she deserved. 'I found out where you lived and whether you needed money. That was all. I had no reason to invade your privacy… then.'

The implications of that—he'd found out how very poor they'd been, and he might suspect her of something underhand, with far less cause than *she* had to believe the worst of him—made her even angrier. But worst of all was the fear. What else had he discovered? Had he sent the money because he knew what happened just before?

Mark spoke when the turbulence in her heart left her too confused to answer. 'You could have changed more than your name.' He looked her right in the eyes. 'I've had trusted friends, lovers and employees sell stories and lies for thousands and feel justified in doing it if I don't give them what they think they deserve. One of my house-keepers stole some personal things from the house and sold them online.'

'I know.' She remembered that story with the same bubbling fury she'd felt when she'd read it three years ago. She'd read almost every article on him, rejoicing in his successes, indignant at what she'd seen as the lies.

Now, seeing the look in his eyes, she saw it as more than a way to feed her fascination with him. She'd fed the media machine, too, by wasting her hard-earned money on the tabloids to clip pictures and articles about him. She'd made his life worse with her silly crush on a famous playboy—like so many girls and women in the country.

And *that* was why he'd had her investigated like everyone else. He couldn't know he'd become so much more than her childhood prince through the years. He'd been her therapy…but she'd healed herself at his expense.

'I understand.' Ashamed of herself, she pushed her chair back. 'I've eaten enough, and it's been a long day. I'll clean up, and head to the cottage and read a book.'

He looked up from his food, his eyes probing without asking, and she knew he saw more than she wanted him to—but when he spoke it wasn't what she'd expected. 'Did my family come to see you today?'

Caught out, she nodded.

'Who?' His voice was grim.

Embarrassed she hadn't seen this coming, she shrugged. 'Your mother, Becky and Katie were waiting when I arrived home,' she said, wondering if he'd catch her slip. After only a few days Mark's warm, beautiful house was her palace, her dream house—had become a word she'd never truly felt in her heart before: *home*. 'They're as nice as I remember.'

'I'll bet they were.' He shook his head. 'I'm sorry.'

About to leave the table, she sat again, arrested by the rueful words. 'For what?'

He didn't look away as he said it. 'For their putting you in the awkward position I know they did simply because Bren told them who you are.'

She felt a stupid blush moving up her cheeks.

'Do I look so weak that a few awkward questions would make me cry?'

'I've rarely met anyone who's been through what you have, done the things you've done, and not merely survived but emerged optimistic—no, joyful.' His tone was curt; he downed the last of his wine before he spoke again. 'You have the deepest sense of self I've ever known in a woman. So why don't you stop avoiding what I haven't asked, and tell me what they said?'

Touched by his opinion of her, she said, 'It's fine, Mark. I handled it all right.' She shot him a glance brimming with mischief. 'They…um… know now to expect the unexpected from me.'

His eyes widened for a moment, before he grinned and leaned his chin on his hands, staring at her with mock-earnestness. 'So, are you involved, gay, or did you really shock them by finding me so unattractive even the money didn't do it for you?'

'The last, of course,' she retorted. 'I said you were downright ugly.'

He threw his head back and burst out laughing.

Delighted, she grinned. This kind of light banter took away all the *don't talk about it*—either about Chloe, or her own secrets.

So many undercurrents—and the fact that he

didn't ask about the things she wanted to keep buried showed her a side of Mark that left the 'Heart of Ice' myth behind. This was the man he could have been had his youth not been stolen by enduring tragedy so young. Yet his experiences had made him the man who now mesmerised her. He looked beautiful, masculine, with a strong sense of decency and self. He seemed so far from the Heart of Ice she wouldn't recognise him from the hundreds of photos with those glamorous women.

How long had it been since he'd laughed like that—as if he'd been let out of a cage?

He pushed back his chair and held out a hand to her. 'Come on, Ginger, let's waltz.'

Her body's reaction was predictable, urgent—but beneath the expected fear a deeper fascination called to her and wouldn't be denied. As fearful as she'd been, dancing in Mark's arms had made her feel like a princess in a fairy-tale....

'Ginger?' She turned her face half away, frowning and peering at him in amused suspicion. 'Is that a reference to my hair or my lack of dancing skills?'

'Whichever you prefer,' he replied without

missing a beat. 'And if you don't like it, too bad. You say things to me no one else would dare, change my house without asking, feed me when I say no and dance in my ballroom without permission.'

'You don't seem very angry about it,' she pointed out.

He shrugged. 'Must be the lasagne and wine mellowing me—or maybe it's your two left feet...Ginger. But we'll get you ready for that wedding.'

She stood, biting the inside of her lip to stop a smile forming, but it did anyway. 'I have to wash up...Fred.' Her hand slipped into his even as she spoke, and she wondered that she'd done it— touched him without its being a traditional expected formality. And she wondered even more that she didn't want to pull away. She felt warm, happy, *safe* with Mark—and she wanted to curl her fingers around his, drink in his skin.

He smiled down at her, those golden-brown eyes warm. 'We can do it later.'

She caught her breath at his casual use of the word. *We* can do it. As if this was their house, their dishes to wash, just like any normal couple. But she could never be part of a normal couple, because she was not and never would be normal. She had to accept that.

Lost in tangled emotions, she barely noticed as Mark drew her back to the ballroom.

'You need a slower song. Try this.' He flicked the stereo on with a remote, and soft strains drifted from the speakers.

He spoke as if she was one of his sisters. He didn't seem bothered by her touch, she thought, fighting a weird mixture of elation and depression. *It's never going to happen, Sylvie. You have to accept it.*

How many years had she been telling herself? And yet being near him, having his hand in hers, the other resting on her waist without intimacy, had gone to her head. *He* had gone to her head. Within only days she was terrified he was already—or still—in her heart, and would always be there. Even if the miracle occurred and she found another man whose touch she could endure, and she married and had ten kids.

No! Infatuation. That's all it is. He's always been a safe love, distant as a star. If he really touched me he'd know what a freak I am….

'Feet in position, facing mine.'

He was so close she could feel the heat of his

body again, could feel the warm rush of his breath on her hair. *Breathe, Sylvie...in, out...*

'This is your dance space; this is mine. Strictly, in a waltz, you never invade that space.'

What if I want to? her heart whispered. *Do you want to as much as I do*? And it shocked and scared her that she really did want to...

'Posture is always straight. Think tall.'

Concentrating on his commands, she drew herself as high as she could.

'Now, look at me.'

That was never a hardship—but would the agonised longing of so many years of dreams show in her eyes? Her lashes lifted, her chin followed, and she drank in the face of the one person whose simple existence had made the un-bearable bearable for so long. Who'd even helped her put the worst nightmare a girl could face behind her because he was alive and she could dream of him and feel as if it had never happened.

His eyes and smile held a strange kind of ten-derness that reassured her. 'There's no need to be embarrassed with me, Sylvie. You're taking care of me, and I'm teaching you how not to land on your butt at your friend's wedding. It's just a deal between old friends. So, let's try the basic moves.

We can go on to something more elegant when you're ready.'

Yes, he was speaking to her as if she was Becky or Katie—and still the rush of heated colour in her face grew, until she felt like one big scarlet neon sign pulsing in the soft-lit old-fashioned ballroom for him to read: *I'm crazy about you.*

She had to stop it—had to stop hoping life and her body could change...

'*One*, two, three,' she counted, her voice strangled with acute humiliation. Because she was a tangled mess of desire and adoration and to him she was merely *his old friend*. She really was safe with him, because he saw her as a little sister. '*One*, two, three.'

His hands tightened on her body. He stepped forward and she moved back. To the count she kept up he moved and she followed, backwards and sideways, slowly round and round in swirls and dips, he looking in her eyes and she into his.

He led her to the middle of the floor, dancing with strict instructions as the next song began.

She should never have given in to temptation when Brenda had called her for the interview and she'd known she'd be working for him. She'd been here not even four days, and she already knew she was in way too deep. She'd thought to be safe because she couldn't bear a man to touch her. But with one touch she'd had her dream come true—Mark had made her normal again, a young woman wanting a man.

Only *one* man…

She was heading for a fall here—big-time.

But tonight, in his arms, resting in his embrace as he led her around the floor, swirling and dipping her in their own private world of moonlight and shadow, feeling graceful and almost *pretty*, she couldn't make herself care.

CHAPTER FOUR

THE next night, when Mark came home, he found her dancing in the ballroom, this time in a simple sundress and low heels.

'I'm trying to practise how it will be for the wedding,' she said, in a tone so serious and so adorable that even with a mountain of paperwork to do he came toward her with an enquiring look. She nodded gratefully, and he took her in his arms. And though he didn't speak to her apart from severe dance instructions, she more than filled the silence.

'How was work?—*one*, two, three—I have a practical stint in hospital next week—*one*, two, three— Orthopaedics. Great—nursing a bunch of raging male hormones in traction, with no one to practise on but us—*one*, two, three—I made *nasi goreng* tonight. Hope you like Malaysian food— *one*, two, three…'

What could a frozen heart *do* with an unpredictable darling who didn't take any amount of hints but just kept on being…adorable?

Invite her to stay for dinner, of course. The Malaysian dish was incredible, she was a sensational cook, and then—again at his instigation—they returned to the ballroom.

She was looking at him as she danced, but he could tell that, though her eyes stayed on him, she was still counting in her head—trying to concentrate on not falling over.

'Trust me, Sylvie, I won't let you fall,' he said, feeling almost tender.

'You won't, but Angelo probably will,' she replied with a sigh. 'He's Scott's best man. He's got two left feet and is so sensitive about his clumsiness he won't take lessons.'

He'd have laughed but for the fact that she sounded almost tragic about it. 'So how will you even get him on the dance floor?'

'That's Sarah's department. Guilt should do it. She introduced Angelo to a dozen girls—including me—until he met Sandi. And now they're the next to walk down the aisle.'

'He won't even take lessons for Sandi?' he asked, wanting to add, *Why didn't* you *like him*?

Because there was no way a guy couldn't be intrigued by this mercurial angel with her pretty face and her heart of gold.

'Sandi loves him as he is, the big goofball.' Sylvie smiled with an affection bordering on tenderness. 'She's banned the waltz from their wedding.'

'She sounds perfect for him.' He was amazed by the shot of wistfulness in him. He didn't *want* to risk his heart again, so why would he deny that joy to others?

She nodded, smiling. 'I'm so glad for them. I like seeing others as happy as they are.'

Was it deliberate, the way she'd said *others* like that?

She was dangerously close to the stereo. He guided her away and, on impulse, dipped her, grinning when she laughed in delight. 'You don't want that for yourself?'

The sudden look on her face—sad and resigned—made him wish he'd never asked.

'There's no use. I don't think I'll ever marry.'

He frowned. That seemed so wrong. If anyone was made for marriage and babies and a happy-ever-after ending it was Sylvie. 'Why?'

'I met my prince years ago, but he loves someone else. I've met a hundred men since, kissed a few, but—' She sighed and shook her head, looking up at him with a smile as bright as the soft shimmering of unshed tears in her old-sherry eyes. 'I have a good job, a lovely waterfront cottage, a pretty decent boss.' Her eyes twinkled in a mercurial mood change only Sylvie could produce. 'And in nine months I'll be a registered nurse. I have a good life. So, can we change the subject before we both become maudlin?'

Something in her resignation bothered him. She was young, pretty and made others happy just by being in the room. The guy lucky enough to marry her would smile until the day he died.

Stop thinking like that!

'We've been dancing for an hour. Maybe we should do the dishes,' he suggested, aiming for friendly distance—hard to do with certain parts of his body still pounding with a weird mixture of joy and want. Kissing Sylvie would be the *happiest*—

Stop it, you dumb jerk!

'Am I doing any better?' she asked, in evident anxiety.

Torn from a fuzzy world of desire, guilt and pain, he saw the look in her eyes and softened. 'You're doing well enough to miss a lesson, since I'm out tomorrow night. We can take it up again

Thursday.' He was already anticipating having his barefoot sprite in his arms again, all soft silkiness and surprisingly addictive conversation.

She turned away, frowning. 'I have midterms at the end of the week. I should probably eat in the cottage and study.'

'Fine,' he said, trying to keep the cold stiffness from his tone. For the first time in years he *wanted* to spend time with a woman, and she was rejecting him.

Perhaps she'd told his family the truth: she *didn't* find him attractive.

'Just so we're clear, Sylvie, I don't seduce my employees. I wasn't trying to hit on you.' Now his voice *was* cold and stiff. He was so unused to rejection these days he didn't take it well. The old shy schoolboy in him would have laughed at the man he'd become.

Still she didn't look at him. 'I know that.' Her hands were so tight-fisted her knuckles showed. Sylvie was made for laughter and sunshine, but right now she was unhappy—and he'd made her feel that way. He'd hurt her, and all she'd said was she needed to study.

He called himself all kinds of names—Heart of Ice being the least of it.

'Go and study, Sylvie. I can clean the kitchen,' he said quietly.

Still looking at the floor, she shook her head. 'It's my job.'

'Your job is what I say it is. You have exams, and I can stack a dishwasher. My mother makes me do it whenever I eat there, to remind me of my roots. I wasn't always an infamous playboy, you know.' And he winked, angling for a smile from her.

For a moment her sweet face lifted, she smiled—and then, as his body began to thrill to it, as he began to feel the happiness he could imbibe by osmosis just by being near her, she turned away.

'Thank you.'

'Thank you, *Mark*,' he replied softly, not knowing why he pushed—but she hadn't said his name for hours, and he wondered why.

Her back still turned from him, she nodded. 'Thank you, Mark.' She looked wilted, a little daisy pushed away from the sunlight. No—she looked as she had the day her mother had died. Brave in the face of suffering, willing to keep trying though she was in pain.

Now, as then, she shamed him with her strength. He had the money, the success, yet she, the housekeeper, knew how to *live* through tragedy, while he'd merely survived. He couldn't be angry with her for showing him all the things he wasn't, because she said nothing. She just *was*.

'Goodnight, Sylvie. Sleep well.'

'Thank you.' There was a little catch in her voice. 'You, too.'

Had he taken his eyes from her for a moment? He must have, because when he looked at where she'd been standing she was gone, leaving only her memory, like an insubstantial dream of a smile, behind her.

The next night, on a date to a movie premiere with all those who were seen or wanted to be seen, he did his part with a woman—Mimi was lively, fun and beautiful—and again he went home after a supper that was awkward instead of an intimate prelude to a night on satin sheets.

He found himself checking for lights in the house or in the cottage when he came in, and felt the bite of disappointment when everything was dark and still.

Leaving a date out of guilt last week he could handle. But this—the *need* to be with her—this situation was becoming dangerous.

Five days later

'Hey, Sylvie,' Mark called as he ran in through the door and up the stairs for a shower. 'I'll be down in twenty.' Unable to sleep much the past three nights, he'd overdone his run this morning in an effort to exhaust himself into sleep tonight. In consequence he was twenty minutes behind schedule, and he had a vital meeting with a conglomerate of auto manufacturers at eleven.

'Okay.'

He stopped in his tracks. Singular as the word was, he felt as if it had raced from her body to his, bouncing off him with its unspoken angst. He almost went back to look at her, to ask—

She'd only shut down if he tried. Last night she'd had something on her mind that had refracted off her body in waves of tension. She'd barely touched him even to dance.

By having a lightning shower, he made it back down in the exact time. He didn't look at her, but he felt the intensity of lockdown in a person he'd never seen lock down in all life had thrown at her.

He wolfed down the muesli, as usual, but kept watching unobtrusively. 'I'm running late,' he said, with a carelessness he hoped wasn't overdone. What was wrong with her? Was she angry at the long-standing date he hadn't been able to break last night? It had been an important event. If he'd backed out, Angie—and the media—would have wanted to know why…

'I noticed.'

Her answer was colourless, so un-Sylvie, he stopped eating and looked at her; she wasn't looking.

'I forgot to ask last night—did you get any exam results back?'

'Two distinctions.'

'That's great—congratulations,' he said, burning to know what was going on in that closed-off section of her. 'Want to celebrate tonight? Fish and chips in the backyard, and another dancing lesson in which I *swear* I won't yell at you?' He laughed.

After a heartbeat, she said, 'No. Thank you,' she added, in obvious afterthought.

'Well, thanks for pretending to want my company at least,' he retorted, stung by the lightning-fast rejection.

'I have plans tonight.'

He looked right at her at last, and saw dark eyes dominating a pale face so white her freckles stood out in stark contrast. She was scrubbing the counter with enough vigour to leave grooves in the granite. She didn't say where she was going, but the plea inside the ongoing silence cried out to him. *Help me.*

'What's up with you today?' He didn't have to try to make it sound indignant; he felt it. He *liked* her, they were friends, and she'd thrown his invitation in his face as if he'd insulted her. 'Is it because I went out last night? I told you we couldn't dance—'

'Your love-life is none of my business.' But though she spoke with hard defiance, she'd stilled so completely he thought she might turn, look at him, say what was really on her mind. 'I have to go. I'll clean up later.' And she was out of the door without her usual cheery *Have a good day*, or tempting him home early with a promise of a mouth-watering dinner.

No smiles. No blushes, adorable comments or deep insights. None of the uniqueness that had kept him at home far more than he ever had been before; nothing that made her *Sylvie*. And it worried him far more than it ought. So he pretended to leave, drove out and came in again through the back door ten minutes later.

She was playing her cleaning music—she had a habit of playing upbeat stuff and dancing as she did the house, he'd caught her at it—but though the music blasted from the stereo, Sylvie was dashing at tears that fell so fast she probably couldn't see the vacuum cleaner she was pushing on the rug.

Go in to her, Prof. She needs you.

The voice of the past, so sure it was right, felt so *real* he didn't hesitate. He strode across the room to where Sylvie cried in silence, yanked the vacuum from her hand, switched it off and pulled her into his arms.

Well, he'd broken her silence at least. Her screams rang right through the house.

Her terror echoed in his heart—and he no longer needed to ask her what was wrong. He was so shocked he didn't even stop her flailing fists as she fought to get away from him, just took the blows. 'You're safe, Sylvie. It's only me,' he murmured as she struggled and whimpered. He held her until her screams became soft sobs that tore at his soul and her head fell to his chest. She laid her cheek against his heart.

'I'm sorry,' she whispered, when she was finally calm.

He shook his head, caressing her hair with a tender hand, hiding the fury within him against the jerk who'd cut her gentle heart into ribbons this way. 'It's okay.' He didn't ask her if she wanted to talk about it, though she desperately needed to talk; any fool could see that. And if he got the name of the—

'It's a bad day today,' she hiccupped.

'Okay.' He knew pushing her would only hurt her more—but he wanted to find out the name of the creep who'd done this to her. He knew she hadn't gone to the authorities, or he'd have seen what had happened on the file his detective had compiled.

She gulped. 'My mother…'

Then he wanted to knock his thick skull against a wall. Of *course*! Fifteen years ago today her mother had died. He knew because in less than a month his own black anniversary would come round: the day he'd become a teenage widower. 'I'm sorry, Sylvie. I should have noticed the date.'

But it couldn't be her mother's death that made her react with such terror to his touch. Not *his* touch—any man's touch… The sense of being haunted, there from the start, gelled to horrifying reality.

He knew her secret, and there was no turning back now.

'How old were you when it happened?' he asked, and though he made it gentle and non-threatening she knew he wasn't talking about this day, this painful anniversary.

She stiffened, pulled away and didn't look at him. 'I don't ask you about Chloe, or why you drink non-alcoholic wine.'

The shock ran through him. She was right—and yet the fact that she knew sent silent shrieks of protest through him. She only had half the story. If she found out the whole truth she'd have the leverage to destroy him.

As if she would. You know her better than that. Help her!

He no longer knew if Chloe spoke to him or if it was his dormant heart coming to life, *believing* in a woman for the first time in what felt like a lifetime. Though he knew he was opening Pandora's Box between them, he obeyed the imperative directive. 'I don't scream when someone touches me.'

She whirled around to face him, her eyes burning. 'And that means you've healed? You think never having any form of meaningful relationship outside of your family, only touching people who mean nothing to you, means you've accepted the past and you're stronger than I am? At least I'm trying to find a real life, and I'm honest when I scream. Who are you lying to more with your image—the world, or yourself?'

She snatched up her tote bag filled with books, ran out through the door and bolted headlong for the bus stop, leaving him with more questions than answers—and the few answers he had were too ugly to deal with.

He barely worked all day for worrying about her. He let Glenn and Pete take the meeting with Macron Motors while he whiled away endless hours tinkering in his lab, making nothing, her words ringing over and over in his head, as loud as her screams.

At least I'm honest...no meaningful relationship...who are you lying to?

That night, there was no music playing when he came home. Dinner was in his slow cooker—a casserole with rice.

And though he knocked on her door it remained closed. Though he kept watching her windows until midnight the lights in the cottage stayed off.

* * *

The next morning all Sylvie wanted to do was leave his breakfast for him and disappear again, but she caught the 5:30 a.m. bus from Drew and Shelley's place, where she'd spent the night playing with baby Nicky while pretending to give Drew and Shelley a night on the town. And her brother, grateful for the time out, knowing the date even if barely remembering their mother, had said nothing about the day or why she was so tense.

She came in when he should have been in the middle of his run, hoping to get everything done and bolt for the cottage—

'Where have you been all night?'

The harsh demand made her halt halfway in the back door, her hand flying to her throat. She stared at him, standing in the alcove between the kitchen and dining room, dressed in jeans and a T-shirt, feet bare, his streaky hair tousled, and wondered how she could find him so beautiful and so frightening at the same moment.

He looked like a storm cloud about to erupt in lightning.

But she was years beyond the terrified, silent acquiescence that had ruined her innocence; she'd never go there again. So she lifted her chin and said calmly, 'I don't think that's any of your business, sir.'

'Don't call me sir.' His jaw worked as he took a step closer. 'Indulge me.'

She faced him down from her eleven-inch disadvantage. 'I don't think so. I'm not one of your sisters.'

'I know that.' His voice sounded as if it had been shoved through a grater, gritty and broken with anger. 'I've been up all night worrying about you.'

She tightened her jaw, refusing to soften. 'That's not my problem. It was your choice. So long as I keep the house clean and provide meals, what I do at night is my business.'

She'd barely finished the words before she was off her feet, in his arms, with his face buried in her hair. 'I know you're still angry with me, but I was worried sick about you,' he growled, holding her with a sweet tenderness that turned his anger into something wonderful to her starved heart; she felt *safe*. 'Don't do that to me again.'

In his arms, feeling his exhaustion and his caring, Sylvie felt her anger melting faster than ice cream on a searing summer's day. She gulped down the hurting lump in her throat, and whispered, 'Okay.'

'I'm an idiot,' he whispered back. 'I should

have known not to push you on that day of all others.'

'Yes, you are—an idiot,' she clarified with twinkling eyes when he pulled back, his eyes filled with questions. 'I'm still mad at you.'

He chuckled and rubbed his unshaven jaw against her cheek, and her heart drank in the intimate punishment as if he'd kissed her. 'Let me make it up to you. A fish and chips and white wine picnic in the backyard tonight.'

Her gaze dropped. 'I—I can't. It's a bad idea.'

'Why?' He lifted her chin, tilting his head so he could see her eyes. 'Is it to do with my reputation, or with what happened to you?'

'Don't.' The word barely made it from her tight throat. 'Please.'

'Who was it?' His voice was rough and tender. 'Who hurt you?'

All she could do was close her eyes and shake her head.

'I trusted you with my pain once,' he said softly, holding her with such gentleness the little hole in her heart cracked open wider and she bled. 'Trust me with yours, Sylvie.'

Overcome with the burden of a secret she'd told no one but Simon, then a thirteen-year-old boy, she laid her head over his heart and shook her head again. Oh, how safe she felt in his arms, and how she *wanted* to open her wounds, to say the words—but the shame, the self-loathing, stopped her mouth like the tape *he'd* threatened to use on her to stop her screaming.

'You said I saved your life—that the money came when you were going under. I sent you the house, the money and trust funds when you were fifteen.' He probed her wound with delicate surgery. 'You were only *fifteen*?'

She couldn't lift her head, even to nod. She could barely breathe the constriction in her chest and throat was so tight.

'Was it a boyfriend?'

Somehow a watery chuckle escaped her. 'Like I ever had time for that.'

The long silence unnerved her. 'A boy at school?'

Her head moved a fraction in negation. She didn't know if he'd feel it as that, or as a shudder.

The quiet felt portentous, because she knew what he was going to say. 'Your father…?'

'No.' Her father had never once laid a hand on her—even when she was naughty or rebelling against her responsibilities, he'd only begged for-

giveness for putting such awful burdens on her. It had always made her feel resentful and strong, glad and furious—had stiffened her spine. Her pride had been inherited from him. Their family would not accept outside help unless they were desperate.

He carried her to the sofa and sat down beside her, his arm circling her shoulders. He lifted her face with his free hand, his eyes not filled with the pity or revulsion she'd dreaded, but with a *caring* that made her feel safe and cherished. 'I want to be your friend, sweetheart, but I can't if you don't let me in.'

'Stop.' Her voice wobbled. 'Please. It's not you. I—I just want to be happy.'

His eyes softened even more. 'We're a pair, aren't we? I bury my past with ice, you do it with a smile. But neither way is working—not for either of us.'

She sighed, fiddling with his T-shirt without thinking of how intimate it was; she felt so secure in his arms. 'I know. But—'

'You're still not ready to talk about it.' He shook his head with a rueful smile. 'Hypocrite,' he whispered, brushing his mouth over her cheek. And the delicate whispers of arousal in her body didn't frighten her, because soft words chanted in her mind: *safe, you're safe with Mark*. 'You keep pushing me out of my hole, but you stay in yours. If you don't talk it out with someone it's going to catch up with you. Your happiness is nothing but pretence until you face your past and leave it behind.'

'Look in the mirror, Hannaford,' she retorted, but its severe effect was ruined by a hiccup. 'What are you doing now?'

'I was talking about the worst parts, not the good parts. Those you keep.' He winked at her, surprising her; she'd expected him to turn dark and cold at her remark. 'I never promised to be consistent.' After a brief hesitation he kissed her cheek again, his mouth a half-inch closer to hers.

She felt his longing as a physical presence inside him. He wanted to kiss her mouth, but he was holding back because he was her boss, because she'd screamed yesterday. She sensed he was giving her the power of choice—but the beauty of his touch overwhelmed her and the ugly past faded to white. With an almost timid eagerness she put her hands on his shoulders and turned her face.

A flood of unbearable bliss filled her being

with the barely there touch of his mouth. Intoxicated by his nearness, by the kiss she'd waited a lifetime to know, she moaned and pulled him closer, her hands winding into his hair.

With a groan he drew her against him, but he kissed her so gently tears flooded her eyes. He knew she couldn't bear passion yet. He caressed her hair, her cheek, her throat, wiped hot tears away with his thumbs, and kissed her over and over, whispering her name. She wanted to cling to him, but she knew this was just for now; he was only hers on borrow from another girl, from a life that could never include her.

Soon, too soon, he'd remember Chloe, and then she'd have to let him go with a smile… But she'd have these few treasured moments in his arms. It wasn't all she'd dreamed of in her girlish fantasies, but it was so much more.

'You're shaking,' he whispered against her mouth, concern shimmering in his eyes.

She lifted one of those trembling hands and put it over his mouth. She didn't know what she was going to say until she said it. 'It's not fear. Not of you. I—I trust you, Mark.' Then she closed her eyes, drawing him closer.

He pulled back, frowning. 'You shouldn't,

Sylvie.' But he caressed her face, his eyes never leaving hers. The desire was there, but far stronger was the storm of self-hate.

'I do. I know you,' she whispered. 'I *know* you—the real you.'

'No, you don't. You don't know the things I've done since you left my life.' Gently he put her back on the sofa and jerked to his feet, pacing the room.

She watched him, aching. 'They're just things. You're still the same person I knew.'

'No. *No.*'

She saw him shudder. 'Do you want to talk…?'

'No.' The word was so harsh she jerked back on the sofa. Seeing it, he sighed and set his jaw for a moment. 'So it's your turn to call me a hypocrite.' But again his voice had come down from the callous tone, was warm and rueful.

Her mouth quirked. 'I was a hypocrite to ask. What a pair we are.' Her eyes twinkled.

His gaze drank her in for a moment, and a thrill ran right through her.

'I'm going to be late for work,' he said quietly, withdrawing without the ice.

He was healing already, becoming the Mark she'd once known….

It's too soon. I can't bear to leave him yet!

The bleeding in her heart grew stronger. She knew if she stayed, she'd have to see him fall in love with a woman truly worthy of him—one who wouldn't bring him public ridicule and shame. He'd probably even invite her to the wedding.

She stood on legs almost too shaky to hold her. 'Only if you still go for your run. We weren't—' She blushed, then said it. 'We weren't kissing that long.'

'No, we weren't.' In a voice gentle yet uncompromising, he went on, 'So, the fish and chips tonight isn't such a bad idea now, is it, Sylvie?'

She bit her lip, fiddling with the throw cover she'd bought for the sofa to relieve the unrelenting green his great-grandparents had obviously liked. 'Not tonight. I wasn't making an excuse. I have three exams this week. I have to pass all of them or risk repeating a year.'

Slowly, he nodded. 'You want to leave this life behind. I don't blame you.'

The deep black of a winter night was in his voice, in his heart. 'Not you. I don't want to leave you behind, or our…friendship,' she faltered.

'Why not? You did before. You never even called to say hi and thanks for the money,' he said, with a quiet harshness that left her shivering.

Her eyes closed. 'That's not fair.' But it *was* fair from his perspective, she realised a moment too late. Why *hadn't* she called?

'Isn't it?'

She felt his eyes boring into her.

'Look at me, Mary.'

Startled by her real name, she obeyed the imperative command.

'I waited for you. I sent you a card with my office and home numbers. I left instructions that if you called the office, day or night, you were to be put right through to me.' He stared at her, hard. 'I waited months to hear from my friend before I gave up.'

She stared at him in horror. 'I was fifteen. I— I didn't think… You'd become so important by then, inventing Howlcat at nineteen…'

The look on his face cut off her protest. 'Yes, I was nineteen—only nineteen—in a life that overwhelmed me…and we were *friends*. I remembered you—Mary.' He didn't say any more. He didn't have to.

He'd been reaching out to her years ago. He'd been giving her help, but also reaching out in the wilderness of his cold isolation, the new and already infamous Heart of Ice crying out for a friend. And she, soaked in gratitude for his rescue, dreaming of seeing him again, still hadn't called, hadn't thanked him.

Hadn't reinstated their friendship because—

The words came out like gravel from a tight throat, from a heart filled with a double-barrelled shame as deadly as any rifle. 'It happened four weeks before...' Her head fell. It was her reason, but no excuse. Mark had saved her from its ever happening again, saved her from a life of degradation—and, lost in the shame she still couldn't conquer, she hadn't felt worthy of speaking to him. She'd come to him in the end, but she'd waited thirteen years too long.

All because of five hundred dollars...

She was snuggled in his arms, hearing his heart beating against her ear, before she knew he'd come to her. 'Sweetheart,' he whispered, 'I'm sorry. I'm sorry I put that guilt on you just because I wanted to see you again. I could have come to you and didn't.' He caressed her hair. 'What is it about us? The best things come at the worst times.'

She nodded against his chest, feeling cherished, feeling *safe*. 'Things can change. We can make it better.'

'Yes, we can.' He spoke with slow wonder, as if she'd delivered a revelation instead of foolish, inadequate words. 'You always see the beginning of a rainbow in a storm cloud.' He dipped down to kiss her, almost heartbreaking in his tenderness.

Warmth as sweet as hot honey ran through her.

Yet she could see the inevitable ending of their unlikely pairing rushing at her like a skier on a downhill run. This couldn't last; they both knew it. Born in the same world, they now stood planets apart.

But he didn't know *why* whatever it was starting between them could never go public. She'd leave both the job and him rather than let him find out the whole truth of what had happened to her thirteen years ago.

CHAPTER FIVE

'HERE you are,' Sylvie said cheerfully, putting a plate loaded with eggs, tomatoes, mushrooms and toast before Mark's bemused gaze. 'I got it all fresh from the market this morning—the lot for ten dollars!'

'You don't work Saturdays,' Mark said, as she put her own plate across from his, as if she'd been invited. 'Why are you in here?'

'Feeding you, silly,' she chided, rolling her eyes as if he should have been expecting it.

And in a way he had. She'd been waiting for him all week when he came home from work; they'd danced, eaten and washed up together— and they'd repeated it last night.

They hadn't kissed again. The situation hadn't been intimate in any way. It felt more as if she was trying to make it up to him for never calling. As if she wanted to be his *friend*.

Sylvie brought coffee mugs to the table, smiling with that sweet pixie-look that made him feel like Scrooge when he argued with her. And she was so *pretty*, in her weird stripy pink and blue pants and her favourite lavender top, with her cheeks flushed from the stove's heat and a bunch of curls escaping from a headband. He didn't *want* to argue.

'I thought you'd like to share my bounty. And, by the way, in most polite societies *thank you* is more acceptable than "Why are you in here?".'

Only Sylvie would call a ten-dollar breakfast bounty—and only she would call him on his lack of manners when she was in *his* house, uninvited, cooking for him barefoot.

'Thank you, Sylvie,' he said, in blatantly sarcastic obedience, hating her pity. 'Thank you for breaking into my home on my day off and inflicting your ten-dollar breakfast on me.'

'And my company, Ice Man. Don't forget I'm inflicting *that* on you, too,' she retorted with a grin, putting the coffeepot on a cork coaster and the milk jug beside it. She leaned over him without coming too close to set two glasses of fresh juice on the table, and her shampoo and talcum powder scent touched him, adding to his inner smile. 'Since you're obviously not in the mood to give thanks for the food, I'll give you the hungry man's prayer: one-two-three-four, praise God, eat more.' She tucked into her food without any more ado. 'Yum, oh, yummy...*eat*,' she ordered, shoving his plate closer with a frown. 'When millions of people are starving around the world, ignoring good food is selfish and arrogant.'

He blinked, wanting to laugh, but he had more self-discipline than that. He wasn't about to let her know that the thought of breakfast without her sunshine and starlight company had sent him on a much longer run than usual this morning—and he hadn't liked the burst of sweet light in him when he'd seen her in here when he came back.

Like the things she'd bought for his home, she'd transplanted herself here, growing as naturally as if she'd always been in his life. And he liked it too much for his peace of mind.

He lifted a forkful to his mouth, groaning in delight at the taste of fresh herbs and just-picked vegetables cooked in butter. 'I can feel my cholesterol count rising as I speak.'

'Once a week won't kill you, Ice Man. Tomorrow I have pancakes for us—a Browning

Sunday special. Organic maple syrup and strawberries to go with them.'

He frowned. 'Don't call me Ice Man.'

She lifted a brow and grinned over a full mouth. When she could speak, she said, 'Then don't play the part with me and I won't.' She waved her fork at him as she ended the mock-lecture. 'You should know by now it's of absolutely no use.'

He filled his mouth with food. No point in saying anything to alienate her when she wouldn't *be* alienated. But what *was* this between them? Not employer and employee, not quite friends.

How did you redefine a relationship that had never had a definition in the first place?

After the next mouthful Sylvie spoke again, her chin on her palm. Her thoughtful tone betokened she was about to say something startling. 'I can't work it out. All the magazines talk about your good looks and smooth charm. Okay, the looks are obvious…a woman would have to blind to miss that and I don't need glasses yet. But where's the charm—or is it that you don't need to waste it on your poor housekeeper?'

He choked on a mushroom and started coughing. She jumped up, ran around the table and began hitting his back in a rhythmic method that actually helped. She handed him his glass of juice when he stopped choking. 'Drink that or you'll get hiccups.'

He broke into helpless laughter, bringing on the prophesied hiccups. She promptly gave him advice on that, too.

'No, don't drink yet! A tic in your diaphragm from the coughing is the cause of it, so…hold the muscle down tight, breathe in and out, same pace again and again….*now* drink all the juice without breathing, then release the breath with the same slow rhythm. That's it. See?' She beamed as the hiccups subsided.

He pushed his plate away and buried his face in his arms. 'Thank you, Sylvie,' he said, aiming for deadpan. But it came out as laughing despair. 'And *that's* why I don't waste my so-called charm on you.'

'Why?' Her curiosity sounded genuine.

He looked up at her—she was too pretty, too genuine, too sweet—too *everything* he couldn't ignore. 'What's the use of trying to charm someone who's stopped me choking and cured my hiccups?'

'You're right, it'd be as useless as the Heart of

Ice routine.' With a thoughtful expression, she added, 'I probably wouldn't like it anyway.'

It was his turn to demand, 'Why not?' Feeling a bit offended that she'd write off his charm without ever having experienced it.

'I've seen the best of you at the hospital and here,' she said simply. 'I like you as you are. Anything else but the real you would feel like a lie.'

Stunned by the truth of it, he saw what she'd probably known from the start: *why* he couldn't say no to her, *why* he couldn't freeze her out or turn her away. She *liked* him. Not Howlcat Man or Heart of Ice, but Mark. What the *hell* did he do with that?

Beneath all his defences he was a simple man. Until now he'd defined his life into two eras. With Chloe he'd been one person. When he'd finally come to terms with losing her and accepted the man he'd become he'd already been the Heart of Ice—unless he was with family and his few trusted friends.

But Sylvie was unique: an old friend who knew him, but didn't know the worst of him, only the best. She'd known him when they were kids, but not again until now. The fact that she wasn't taken in by the Heart of Ice routine left him confused, as if she'd taken away the comforting boundaries and categories he put people in—including himself.

So now, though he knew he should push her away, he heard himself saying, 'Thank you,' and he sounded as touched as he felt. She *liked* him.

For the first time in half an hour she wasn't cheeky or shocking him with her pronouncements. Her smile was as soft as starlight, her eyes as comforting as a fire in winter. 'You're welcome, Mark.'

Why her honesty scared him down to his soul he didn't know—or maybe he did, which was why he scraped back his chair and said, 'I have to get ready. I have a lunch date.'

'Me, too,' she said in cute surprise, as if they shared a secret. 'Have fun on yours. Is she nice?'

'She's great,' he replied on auto-pilot, darkness slamming down on him. Sylvie was going on a date? With whom? What was he like? Was he good enough for her? Would he make her happy?

It's none of your business, Hannaford.

He took his plate, glass and mug to the counter, rinsed them and stacked them in the dishwasher as if he wasn't burning to ask. And he hadn't lied: *she* was his boat, and he was keeping his usual Saturday date with her. For years *Harbour Girl* had been his refuge, his place to be alone, to be Mark. No woman had ever been on her.

And now the one day he'd been tempted to ask a woman to come with him she had a date.

Sylvie was home again before four, ready to face another Saturday night alone. Honestly, why had she bothered? Rob, her lunch date, a junior doctor at the hospital where she'd done her last practical stint, was a terrific guy with a nice personality—but she'd only wanted to find him a nice girl who'd *see* him.

With a sigh, she dragged her books from the cottage and set them on Mark's coffee table. She put on his stereo, curled up on his lovely oak and tapestry sofa and prepared to study human biology. Two final exams to go; she might as well be prepared.

'What are you doing here?'

She squealed and jumped, dropping her notes in a jumbled mess over the table and floor. She glared up at Mark, standing on the landing between floors, dressed in shorts and a T-shirt, and felt her breath catch. Those long, muscled, tanned legs… '*Now* look what you made me do,' she complained, and to cover her blushing cheeks and racing heart she leaned over to gather them up.

He strolled down, crouched beside her and helped her pick up the papers, put them in order, and handed the bunch to her. 'You shouldn't lean so far over in a top like that,' he remarked in a neutral tone.

She dropped the papers again as she yanked her top up. 'I don't have enough there to make a cleavage,' she snapped, her cheeks on fire.

'Small or large doesn't matter; they still dominate the male hormonal reaction. We poor men are slaves to what we see—or want to see.' He handed the papers to her again—and though he wasn't looking *there* her heart was still in her throat.

Panic clawed at the sweet bud of excitement in her—but to her shock the arousal fought back and was winning. She lost her breath and the ability to speak, and sat there waiting for him to look again, to make a move, to touch her....

'So, why aren't you still on your date?'

She felt like a hot air balloon shot down by a bazooka of ice. 'Nice guy. Not my type,' she said with a shrug. No point in saying *none of your business* when she was in his house without excuse. 'What about you?'

'Unsatisfying.'

The curt tone made her heart kick up yet another notch. 'What was wrong with her?'

'Nothing wrong with her. It's me.' He didn't look at her. 'She wasn't the one I wanted to be with.'

Chloe.

She lowered her gaze, too fascinated by the simple movement of his mouth, wishing it was on hers. 'I'm sorry,' she said softly, hating the dark jealousy in her. Hating that her competition was a dead girl he couldn't forget.

Competition? The thought made her freeze inside. She'd come here expecting nothing, hoping for nothing for herself— *And she's lying to herself again, folks.*

'So do something about it.'

Confused, she glanced up, and was caught by the half-smile lurking about that riveting mouth. 'What?'

'It's your fault I was with my favourite Saturday date and could only think *Sylvie would love to be here.*' Still wearing that enigmatic smile, he held out a hand to her. 'So, if you have a few hours you can take off studying, come with me. I'll introduce you to my favourite Saturday girl.'

Rearing back, she stared at him, caught between another bout of horrifying jealousy and wondering if he'd lost his mind. 'Won't the lady think that's a bit on the sick side?' *And won't it make the tabloids?*

It was the one thing she was doing her utmost to avoid in this crazy thing between them—past and present, shadow and sunlight, two people who knew the darkest of each other's souls and so little more. If Mark ever discovered her secret, she'd want to curl up in a corner and die.

He lifted a brow. 'She won't think a thing about it.' He pointed out through the back windows. '*Harbour Girl* has been my regular Saturday afternoon date for five years.'

Confused, she turned her head, and saw a small white yacht with pink edging bobbing on the water at the end of his private jetty.

A vision flashed into her mind: Chloe had always had a little bit of that shade of pink on her somewhere. She'd had a pink knitted cap on the day she'd asked Sylvie for her promise. *Make him happy again, Mary. He'll need a friend.*

She'd never been on a yacht….

She saw that irresistible smile and the strong brown hand held out to her—and, caught between the rock of desire and a fast-falling heart and the hard place of a promise to a dead girl, she did the only thing she could: she put her hand in Mark's.

She was already dressed in her favourite shorts and top, which he deemed appropriate for sailing, but he sent her into the cottage for a pair of rubber-soled shoes and a hat. Within five minutes they were on *Harbour Girl*.

She sat down and hung on to a rail as he released the line, the sails caught the wind, and the boat moved into deeper waters.

'Come here,' he called, beckoning to her.

The boat was pitching with the small waves racing to shore. 'I don't think so.' She kept a tight hold on the rail.

'We're barely moving. People have probably pushed you harder when the Manly ferry is in the Heads.'

Giving in with a loud sigh, she released her death grip on the rail and, shuffling foot by foot, made it to him. 'Well?' she demanded, caught between delight at the new experience and fear of falling overboard.

'You look terrified. I thought you'd like the experience.' He tilted his head, studying her. 'So, is it the boat or my sailing skills you don't trust?'

'It's the size of the thing. It's so small, the rails

are low, and—I can't swim. I never learned,' she blurted, feeling the heat scalding her cheeks. 'If I fall overboard either I die and you lose a house-keeper, or you dive in after me and you could lose your boat.'

His eyes softened. 'That's easily fixed. Come here.' He reached back and pulled a life jacket from behind him. 'This is why I called you back here—that and sunscreen.'

He pulled off her hat and pulled the life jacket on, tying it less tightly than her insecurity wanted—but then she wouldn't be able to breathe. Then she forgot all about her fears when he began smoothing sunscreen on her arms and shoulders in soft, rhythmic strokes that left her quivering inside—and not with fear.

'Um, thank you.'

'You're so fair, an hour in this heat will roast you.'

His practicality made her want to sigh. Why did his simplest touch do so *much* to her, and yet he seemed so unaffected?

'I can do it,' she protested with a breathless note she despised. Why was it every man's touch made her terrified except the one man who was as far out of her reach as the moon?

'That would necessitate letting go of the rail—and I think I'd have to break your bones to force that.' He laughed.

She had to admit he was right. About to retort, aching to show him how much of a woman she was beneath the façade, she closed her mouth—because for the third time in a couple of minutes he was laughing.

'He's barely laughed in years,' Brenda had told her.

So what if he laughed at her expense? It was what she was here for, right? To give him laughter and love and happily ever after—only not with her. So what did it matter how he saw her? She was his pit-stop on the way to life.

'So, where are we headed, Captain?' she asked in a jaunty tone. The smile of hidden sadness, the tears of a clown—but if it helped him live again she'd do it.

'Brooklyn's quite a way, but if you have the time there's warm, calm pockets of water there to learn to swim. Especially in the evening, when it's quiet.' He shot her an enquiring glance.

'If it's all the same to you I'd rather learn somewhere a bit less—less deep. Like a kiddie pool.'

He tipped up her chin with a finger. 'You aren't that little, or that young.'

'I know.' Her body quivered with the simple touch, with the step closer. He was only a breath or two away. 'Old enough to vote, to work, to marry and have half a dozen kids,' she retorted, her heart beating hard and her fingers trembling.

His eyes roamed her face. The softness had a touch of desire—and her pulse went into overdrive.

'Is that how many you want?'

Without warning the shutters slammed over her soul. She felt her right shoulder lift and hunch. 'I did as a child: the prince, the palace, half a dozen beautifully behaved and appropriately royal children. What girl doesn't dream of the whole shebang?'

'Then leave the kiddie pool for them, when you marry your prince and the kids come. You're a woman who's missed the joy of swimming in the ocean. Come to Brooklyn and swim with me. I'll be with you all the way. I won't let you drown. Trust me, Sylvie,' he said softly, close enough to touch, his breath warm and smelling of mocha coffee.

She all but melted at his feet. 'I do,' she whispered, her eyes enormous as she drank in his face—the high cheekbones, the bump on his nose, the crooked smile and the eyes she'd been swimming in for so long she could barely remember a time she hadn't. 'I don't have my swimmers on.'

His smile grew. 'Me neither, since I wasn't planning on a swim today. We'll just wear what we have on. I have towels, though, and some sandwiches and hot chocolate mix in the galley. We'll eat on deck after our swim to dry off and sail home tonight.'

A boating adventure with Mark; swimming and a picnic and a night sail home….

'All right,' she whispered. Where had her voice gone? Out into the harbour along with her good sense, no doubt. Thrown overboard by the one word she should never allow when it came to him.

Hope.

CHAPTER SIX

'I CAN'T. It's too deep,' Sylvie babbled for the fifth time.

She stood beside Mark at the edge of the yacht, where he'd dropped the ladder, looking down at the lapping water as if there were dozens of hungry crocs and sharks circling below her. Then she looked at him helplessly. 'I just can't.'

She was shaking, and her tremors were real.

Mark could see she'd gone as far as she could on her own. She'd taken the wheel as he trimmed the lines, she'd learned to avoid the boom as she crossed the boat—she'd even let go of the side rail and begun to run. She'd loved the sunshine on her face and the salt wind in her hair, even laughed at the splashes of water drenching her when they reached the Heads, the notorious rough patch of water heading to Manly. She'd landed on her butt more than once and didn't care.

She'd had a ball today. He knew that. She'd let go of her fears and enjoyed the adventure. But that was with the life jacket tied securely around her. Now her face was so white her freckles stood out in sharp contrast. Her courage had left her.

Maybe he was going too far, but he *knew* that if he could get her into the water…

'Here.' He climbed down the ladder and jumped in, feeling the summer-warm water envelop him like a lover's arms—and why he always had to think of lovers when he was with Sylvie he didn't know. He could control all but the most fleeting lust with all women but the one who was way off-limits. She was too high above him, too pure and giving for damaged goods like him.

To banish the thought, even knowing he was flying right into a no-go zone, he lifted his arms. 'Come down to me.'

Her face so white her eyes stood out in sharp contrast to the pale skin, she shook her head, edging back.

At this point he knew he should stop—but something perverse forced him to try one more time. 'Just shut your eyes, hold your breath and jump. I'll catch you. I promise,' he said with gentle persuasiveness. Was he pushing for her sake, or because he wanted to feel her in his arms, warm and slippery, in the buoyant ocean? 'I know you're scared, but you'll never conquer it unless you try. You'll spend your life terrified of the unknown.'

As he'd hoped, his reference to fear did it. As her predictable pride kicked in, a wave of colour hit her cheeks, she dragged in quick, hard breaths, and she screwed her eyes tight shut. Instead of climbing down the ladder, she stepped off the edge.

A moment later his arms were full of the forbidden; the satin skin of her bare legs flew past him. He wrapped his arms around her waist before she could go under and panic. 'That's it, Sylvie. Hold on to me—not so tight. I need to breathe,' he mock-complained to make her laugh, loving the feel of her arms wrapped around him so close her face was buried in his neck.

She'd never let him this close to her before. Even when they'd kissed he'd sensed part of her holding back, watching, waiting for the panic to kick in. But right now she trusted him completely—she had no choice.

Could she feel what she was doing to him? That he was more aroused than he'd felt since his teens and she was fully clothed?

You're her boss. You're teaching her to swim. Get over it!

'It's cold,' she muttered near his ear, her teeth chattering.

He held her against him, trying to reassure her, to make her feel safe. Trying to ignore his rebel body's *I've got to have her* response he couldn't shut down. 'That's fear speaking. It's really warm.'

'No, it's freezing! I want to get out!' she cried, suddenly struggling against him.

Was it really the cold that caused her terror? Or had she felt his body's reaction to the sweetest armful of woman he'd felt in half a lifetime?

To test her, he said softly, 'Come on, my fearless girl, you took on the Heart of Ice and won a job and a friend. A little water can't beat you, surely?'

She stiffened; he literally felt her spine moving tight into place. Her reliable pride kicked in once more and she stopped moving—apart from her feet, kicking to stay up in natural reaction.

'Well?' She spoke through what sounded like lockjaw, but she wasn't giving in. She'd fight her fear to the end now.

He laughed, low and soft. 'Now you release

your stranglehold on me, take my hand, lift your body to the top of the water and float.'

'I can float,' she retorted, with that adorable indignation he loved to see. 'Well…in a bathtub,' she amended, blushing.

In the glow of her blush he saw a vision of her sweetly naked, floating in a hot tub, with her lovely curling hair rippling across the water like a pillow….

He gritted his teeth, breathed out and made himself smile. 'Salt water's a little different to the bath. Here—let me show you.' He turned her body with a hand at her back.

Then he lifted her so she floated on the bobbing water. He disciplined his eyes to remain on her feet, hands and face. Looking anywhere else left him feeling as if he was the one needing the life jacket. Her hair spread across the warm salt water in rippling dark waves, and her chest rose and fell against his skin with every anxious breath.

He held her hand for reassurance as he taught her first to float, then to turn and kick. She floated well, and learned to swim basic strokes on her back. She was awkward with freestyle—principally because she wouldn't let go of his hand—and began to sink every time she even thought of letting him go. So he tried breaststroke, with far greater success, because he could follow her arm movements without head-butting her.

'You're a natural,' he told her half an hour later, when he could see she was flagging and they climbed back on the deck to dry. 'You'll be swimming in no time.'

Her cheeks glowed with pleasure. 'Once I learned how to do it I didn't want to stop. I didn't know it would feel like that.'

She took the towel he handed her, then bent over and alternately shook and squeezed the water from her hair. She undid her shirt by two buttons, squeezed that out, too, and tied it in a knot above her navel. Without even looking at him, she squeezed out her shorts, too, bending over a little as she did.

Nothing she did was provocative, yet Mark's mouth was dry and his heart was pounding like a jackhammer. He wanted to turn away, to give her privacy—how wrong was it for him to lust over an old friend this way?—but he couldn't make his body obey his will. How did she make him want her so much, light up his inner darkness without trying?

'Didn't know it would feel like what?' He

heard the husky note in his voice, and threw up a fast prayer she wouldn't recognise it for the yearning it was.

That was the worst of it. Simple lust he could handle. This was more—it was way too much. Why was he standing here, dripping water, fascinated by a woman he couldn't slake himself with and walk away?

'So free, so joyous,' she answered in a dreamy voice that heightened his sense of danger to the red zone. 'Like we were alone in the world, surrounded by warm water and sun and…'

She turned her face to share her joy. He masked the intensity of his reaction too slow, and her words dried up.

Her eyes were enormous as she stared at him, her sweet skin dappled with salt water and sunshine. She wet her mouth and he groaned quietly.

'Listen to me talking like I'm some kind of poet. Why didn't you tell me to be…?' She swallowed, blinked and stepped back. 'I must have swallowed too much sea water. I need a drink.'

She fled down the stairs to the galley.

Mark was left standing on the deck, heart pounding, mouth dry, body aching. It had come to this—the famed playboy and Heart of Ice, the man who'd felt *nothing* for almost half his life, who'd played the game with some of the most beautiful women in the world, reduced to the level of any other dumb jerk in the world, in thrall to the one woman he couldn't have.

Despite her kissing him last week, the complete fear in her reaction just now couldn't be faked. He'd *frightened* her with his feelings…and he *terrified* himself.

As he debated with himself over the wisdom of following her, he frowned. He'd frightened her with a simple look, yet she'd trusted him to touch her until then—and the *why* of her trust suddenly made sense: he'd touched her, held her, *before* what had happened to her.

The ugly suspicion he hadn't wanted to think about the other day crystallised to bleak knowledge: if she was going to heal, it was up to him to do it.

He followed her down a few minutes later.

What would he think of her? Would he have seen she was as aroused as she was terrified? Did he think her a scared doe, bolting at the first scent of danger?

'I hope you left some water for me. You've been down here long enough to fill a camel's hump.'

The total normality in his tone, as if nothing had happened, forced a rush of breath from her lungs. She didn't know she'd been holding it. 'Oh, there's a drop or two.' Her voice was rusty, as if she hadn't used it in days. As if she hadn't been laughing and chattering all afternoon with each new discovery on the boat.

'Good.' He came into the galley, poured from the bottle into a glass, and drank long and thirstily, rivulets of sea water trickling down the rough brown skin of his throat.

Suddenly she needed more water. Lots of water.

She turned to the water bottle, heaving in a dry breath, her whole body aching to see that look on his face again and this time to *do* something about it.

Yeah, you'll do the same old thing. Run.

Did she seem as crazy to him as she did to herself? Her seesawing emotions were impossible to control. During all the years he'd been her therapy her love and desire for him had been *safe*—because he'd been as distant as the moon.

Even when she'd come here she hadn't felt threatened, because a man like Mark—rich, handsome, playing the field—couldn't possibly find a tiny china doll attractive.

But he did…or at least he had for a moment. She didn't count the kisses the other day which he'd meant in comfort—she'd known that all along. But today he'd seen her as a woman, had looked at her with aching desire…and that had resurrected all her fears that her secret would come to the surface. Being with a man as intensely media-magnetic as Mark would ensure the truth would out some day. It would destroy the boys, and Mark, too—and it would risk everything she'd planned for her future.

She should never have come today. What if the media—?

'Are you hungry? I have a pack of sandwiches I bought at a local deli this morning.' He reached over her in the cramped room to pick up a basket. 'Let's head up on deck. We can dry off as we eat.' He turned to the stairs.

He was talking to her as if she was a sister again—and she felt the exact same mixture of relief and resentment as the last time. She released another breath, said, 'Lead the way, boss-man,' and headed for the stairs.

'Don't call me that!' But the words were teasing. 'Ginger.'

She laughed, and followed him up to the deck.

The sun was beginning to sink; the soft rose hue of its setting touched the edges of the lapping waves with gentle fire. She sank onto one of the towels he'd laid over a blanket and accepted the glass he held out to her, giving a smile that felt uncertain.

'It's nothing fancy—sandwiches and wine.' He looked tense as he said it. 'I hope you like white.'

'I do.' She sipped at the wine and again tasted the difference. But if she kept her secrets he had the right to his. 'It's fresh—perfect for the outdoors.' She reached into the basket. 'I'm starving, and—'

He relaxed and laughed. 'I know—we can't waste a scrap.' He unwrapped a sandwich. 'So, tell me what you plan to do with your degree when you're done. What branch of nursing do you want to go into?'

She dragged in a breath, knowing what would happen as she said it. 'Terminal illnesses,' she said quietly. 'I've already applied for St Agatha's. They've accepted me—contingent on my passing all subjects, of course.'

He stiffened. 'I see.'

Her eyes met his. 'You know how it is, Mark. Doctors and nurses do their best, but they're so busy with all their patients. Until you've lived through the slow death of a loved one you don't realise the empathy is missing. The families of the dying *need* that—just as we needed it. But we were kids, and back then they didn't think to provide grief counselling for the children. We were lucky we found what we needed in each other.'

'Until you left.' He put down his sandwich. 'I was so damn *alone* after you went, just watching her die.'

Tender compassion filled her for the strong, loving boy left alone with his loss. Forgetting her fears, she laid a hand over his. 'I'm so sorry. I had you when I needed you most. I should have come, should have called—'

He gave her a humourless smile. 'You were a girl with more than enough to do. If only you could do it all. You had far more on your plate than I did after she was gone.'

He was right. Until now she hadn't thought of it that way, but after Chloe's death he'd probably fallen into a gaping hole of *nothing*. She'd had years of being there for her family—having a reason to get up every day, a higher purpose in everything she did—but he'd had nothing. Now she understood why, when Joel had gone off to university, it had seemed the perfect time to fulfil her promise to Chloe and come back into Mark's life: she'd needed to fill the gap.

Mark had never learned how to do that. He'd filled it with the work that had brought him fame and fortune but only temporary satisfaction; with women who meant nothing. He'd had his family, but they *worried* about him rather than helping him to find a new purpose in life.

He'd had half a lifetime of Chloe always being beside him; after five years of being her significant other, her support, her friend and finally her husband, loving her through her illness, he must have felt like a rudderless ship after she'd died. No wonder he'd thrown himself into his inventions, done so much through the years….

'I wish you'd come to see me,' she said softly, feeling her way. 'There were times I felt so alone, so weighed down I could scream. Every time I had a free hour Joel or Drew would cry, or Dad would get sick. Simon did what he could to help me, but he was the clever one, the one who was going to save the family, so he had to be free to study.' She frowned, looking out over the water. 'I used to think of you as I rocked Joel to sleep at night. I thought of you when the kids at school thought I was a freak and I spent lunch hours with my dreams. You made everything bearable for me even when you weren't there any more.'

After a long moment in which the only sound was a seagull's cawing cry he said, 'I thought of you, too. I would have come, but I—' He closed his eyes, shook his head. Whatever he'd been going to say was still too painful for him.

'You were my best friend.' She bit her lip as she made the admission. 'Always, when I felt lost or alone or scared, I remembered how you held me that day, and I imagined you were there, with your arms held out to me.'

He'd buried his face in the crook of his elbow, his knees holding him up. 'I'm nobody's hero, Sylvie. God help me, I couldn't even save myself.'

She nodded, accepting the meaning behind his words without letting him know she suspected his secret. 'But you still saved me,' she said quietly.

He made a deprecatory gesture. 'Just money.'

'A home when we were about to be thrown out

of it. A trust fund for the boys that saw them through university—and for me…' She choked, unable to say it. 'You'll never know what you've been to me, Mark—more than just the money. *You.*'

He shook the head still resting in his arms, as if the load he carried was too heavy for him to bear.

A little hole in the dam of her bursting heart cracked open. 'You,' she repeated, and as lost in compassion as he was in despair of the past, she leaned over, lifted his face and brushed her lips over his. 'God only knows what I would have become if not for you. You saved my life. Thank you, Mark. *Thank you.*' With tears in her eyes she kissed him again, filled with gratitude and drenching sweetness, then she drew back as unbearable beauty hit her like a bullet to the heart. She'd kissed him, and it made her feel aroused and so very *beautiful*….

The sun fell to the horizon beyond the open sea, deepening the sky above them to lavender and the water to grey-black as he stared at her in silence. Then he leaned forward, brushing his mouth over hers like moth's wings, tender and unsure.

He knew something was wrong and he gave her

the choice: draw back or accept. But she had *no* choice; the sweet lassitude filling her held her in chains. Terrified, longing, she took her turn again, leaning into him, drinking in the hot summer salt scent of him as her mouth moved on his, over and over. Feather-soft tastes of paradise forbidden….

They didn't touch. Neither deepened the kisses. They never descended to passion, but it remained there, hovering between them unspoken. Faerie kisses filled their souls as, through speaking of the past and yet leaving so much unsaid, childhood friends and new acquaintances became something more. Barely moving, boss and employee crossed the line, both knowing this time they couldn't go back, but needing each other too much to stop. Both held hostage to the past, unable to open up to anyone else, they trusted the people they'd once been and opened unseen gates to trusting who they were now.

Strange to know so much about him and yet barely know him at all….

And then he pulled away, put his food back in the basket, downed the wine and stood, lifting her to her feet, as well. 'We should go.'

Though his voice wasn't cold, it was quiet. Too

quiet—and the words hovered around them unspoken, like everything else today, a memory beautiful and poignant, but leaving them both feeling cold and dead.

Night fell, and it was as if he had taken part of it and wrapped it around him, lifting the draw-bridge to his heart, locking himself in cold darkness. Sylvie grieved in silence for something precious she hadn't truly had to lose.

After a nightmare day at work, Mark came in a few minutes before midnight on Monday night to find the lights on. He frowned, entering the back way, and though he was getting used to it now he still took a deep breath, inhaling that amazing, uplifting scent again.

The oven was on low. Flowers picked from his garden stood in a vase on the table—

And Sylvie was curled up sleeping on his sofa.

He came towards her, the smile growing; she was so *beautiful* like that, in shorts and a T-shirt obviously inherited from a brother, miles too big and advertising a heavy-metal rock band. Her hair was a tangled mess, her hand under a cheek flushed with sleep—and she did more to him, body and heart, than the glamour of any woman he'd touched in half a lifetime.

He'd tried to avoid her. He'd gone out all day yesterday, spoken to her as little as possible this morning. But no matter what barriers he put up she slipped under his false cold skin and warmed him with her presence, her sunshine smile. She made the women he'd dated until now seem hard and callous with her sweet, pretty freckled face and her shining honesty.

Still smiling, he bent to her. 'Sylvie.'

'No,' she mumbled, and flipped over.

He chuckled. 'Sylvie, wake up.'

'Go *away*, Simon.' She sighed and curled up again.

Giving up on waking her, he lifted her in his arms. He loved the way she snuggled into him, as though even in sleep she knew who he was and trusted him.

Inhaling the scent of her—sweet flowers and shampoo—moving his fingers like a whisper against her silky skin, he carried her to the cottage, opened the door—

He stopped after a single step inside. Horrified, he looked around.

After her demand that he never enter her cottage he'd expected simple furnishings—but not this. *She had nothing but a mattress, a rug and an old wardrobe.*

No TV. No fridge or microwave. No furniture. Not even second-hand stuff. Just that rug on the floor covered with books. A picture of her with her brothers and one of her parents hung on the back living room wall, but that was all.

No wonder she practically lived in the main house and chose to study there. No wonder she danced to her music on his stereo. She had nothing…*nothing*. And still she'd bought presents to make *his* house, already magnificent, more of a home.

He should have known! It was so ridiculous and yet so *Sylvie*. Of course the girl he'd known would become a woman who'd spend her hard-earned money to buy gifts for a lone wolf multi-millionaire when she had nothing herself. He'd bet his entire fortune that her brothers lived in well-supplied homes filled with furniture *she'd* given them, and that she always visited them so they wouldn't know the truth.

What debt was she paying off that her brothers—

one of whom a resident doctor, earning reasonable money—didn't know about?

Her father's medical bills. He'd give his entire fortune away if he was wrong.

Giving in to the temptation gnawing at him body and soul, he bent and kissed the flushed cheek, inhaled the uplifting, intoxicating scent of her. Just shampoo and five-dollar cologne. Yet because it was *her* it was beautiful. He turned his face and touched his lips to hers, as he'd done on the boat... He touched, then brushed over her mouth with his, once, twice and deepened it so tenderly he hoped it wouldn't wake her.

But after a few moments a soft sigh filled his mouth, fluttering fingers touched his face, and sleeping lips kissed his. Dreaming kisses filled with the wonder and joy he could have shared with her for life.

Once upon a time.

When he finally stopped, a soft whisper touched his mouth. *'Mark.'* Just his name, yet so filled with longing that unexpected pain shafted through him.

After a long time he carried her back into the main house. He couldn't leave her here. Step one in Sylvie's life change was about to begin. He knew what he had to do—and he prayed he was right and he'd found the only way to make her accept what he had to give.

When the alarm went off the next morning, Sylvie woke up with a sense of luxurious confusion. She scrunched up her closed eyes and stretched, feeling a sweet, shuddering *ah* of relief, not needing to work out the kinks in her back and neck.

Her bed was *comfortable*. And the alarm didn't play the radio, but made a muted beeping sound.

Her eyes flew open. From cleaning the house, she knew exactly where she was: one of Mark's spare rooms. The bed was a king single, with solid bedposts and rail slats—good, solid forties furniture. The mattress was thick and cloud-soft.

Still dressed in the shorts and T-shirt of the night before, she leaped to her feet, turned off the alarm—it was six-thirty-five!—stripped the bed of its lovely pure cotton percale sheets for washing, and headed down the stairs.

He was dressed, seated at the table and eating the last remnants of the muesli she'd made the day before. 'Morning,' he greeted her, with a cheerfulness that seemed overdone to her paranoid ears. 'I'd ask if you slept well, but I know you did judging by the snoring.'

Arrested despite herself, she blushed. 'I do *not* snore.'

'No—you do this funny triple-catch of your breath. Huh, huh, *huh*.' He made the sound, each *huh* higher-pitched than the last.

She stopped where she stood, glowering but un-decided. 'Why did I wake up in your spare room?'

He kept eating, and turned a page of the morning paper and read while he chewed and swallowed. Sylvie fumed.

'Well, you told me to stay out of your place. I tried shaking you, but you told me to go away—oh, and you called me Simon.' He looked up and grinned. 'Did he have the same trouble waking you that I did?'

She thought of her brother's complaints when she'd been studying for her Higher School Certificate and had commonly fallen asleep on the old sofa. *'You sleep like the dead,'* he'd always said when she woke up, being dragged by her feet through the hallway to her room. Lucky for her they hadn't had a staircase, or she'd probably have had concussion on a regular basis.

'You carried me to—to the room?' She felt her cheeks and throat heat up.

He shrugged. 'It wasn't hard. You really don't weigh much, do you?' He turned another page. 'By the way, I'll be home early tonight. We have to go out.'

Delight streaked through her. 'We do?' she asked shyly, forgetting to ask why he'd set her alarm for six-thirty instead of five-thirty.

He nodded, his attention absorbed in the international news pages. 'Well, it's either that or give you the ten thousand dollars I owe you up-front.'

'Ten—' she choked on the words. *Ten thousand dollars*. And he'd said it as if it was nothing. It was more than she'd seen or had in her life—for her own trust fund had gone on medicines for her dying father. Thoroughly intrigued, she demanded, 'You owe me money? What for?'

His answer was vague as he kept on reading. 'My lawyer went over your contract and he'd forgotten the clause regarding a furnished residence in the terms. I'd forgotten too, because the last three housekeepers brought their own stuff and took the cash instead.'

She shook her head, trying to clear it. 'I don't understand. Why are we going out?'

'Pierson Brothers is having a private pre-stock-take sale tonight for their special customers. I have to go personally to get the bargains.' He looked up and smiled, still in a distracted way. 'I'd appreciate it if you came.'

Now she was really suspicious. 'Why?'

He sighed. 'You commented on my homey, old-fashioned furniture—that's because it's all my grandparents' stuff; they left it to me in their will. I don't know what you want for your place, but since it's going to be yours for the time being, you might as well pick what you like.' He returned to the newspaper. 'If you don't want to bother I could ask one of the girls, but they'd spend all their time pumping me about you—'

'I get it.' She lifted a hand, unable to argue with his logic—but she'd be checking her copy of her contract when he was gone. 'I'll come.'

'Good.' His gaze remained on the paper but she felt something simmering in him—an emotion she couldn't identify. 'Be ready at six. We can eat out after. What do you like?'

Long moments ticked on the wall clock before she answered. 'I don't have a dress suitable for the kind of places you go to...*sir*. And I have no desire to be on page three tomorrow as your latest squeeze.'

His brows snapped together. 'Who do you think you're speaking to? Some prince of the blood? I grew up as you did, Sylvie, and I haven't forgotten it even if you have. I still love a burger or a kebab, and I eat Chinese takeout regularly.'

She felt her stupid cheeks heating up again. Her suspicions on why he'd brought the entire subject up in the first place hadn't abated, but there was no way she could ask now without seeming churlish. 'I'm sorry, Mark. That was uncalled-for.'

He nodded. 'So, what food do you like?'

'I like anything, and I love to try new foods,' she offered, feeling embarrassed even giving her opinion to him after the way he'd put her in her place.

'Excellent. I know a great place not far from Taylor Square. It's a Spanish place—lively and fun when they start the dancing.' He gave a careless shrug. 'We could try waltzing to a Salsa beat. It'd be good practice for you.'

In his arms, doing a sensuous Latin American dance…

Oh, her ridiculous cheeks—would they never

stop giving her away? Why not put up a sign saying *Woman with intense crush on her boss*? 'How dressy should I be?'

'A simple dress will be fine, but wear heels if we're going to dance. You need to practise in what you'll be wearing for the wedding.'

He didn't look up, didn't see her hot cheeks or respond to the breathlessness in her tone. He spoke as if he'd asked her to polish the floors again.

'All right,' she replied, squashing a ridiculous urge to sigh.

He pushed his chair back. 'Have a good day at college.'

'You too,' she called, caught up in an absurd mixture of trepidation and excitement. She was going on a second date—well, a second *non-date*—with him.

A single backwards wave was Mark's only answer, and in his avoidance of speaking to her as normal she felt a chill as cold as his face had been when he'd walked out the door.

CHAPTER SEVEN

I DON'T seduce my employees.

But that didn't mean he hadn't thought about it constantly since that first kiss. It had grown to unbearable proportions since smoothing sunscreen over her silky skin, holding her body against his in the water. Each day felt like torture—trying to treat her like a sister when all he ached to do was sweep her into his arms and carry her to his bed. Not to a hotel, to *his* bed—and the worst part was it didn't even terrify him. She was in his life already; she *knew* him, cared about *Mark*, and the thought of having her in his bed was as natural as taking her to a hotel was alien.

He also thought constantly about making her life better. He could still taste the exquisite relief when she'd agreed to shop with him...and when she clearly hadn't read her contract thoroughly before he'd replaced it at 5:00 a.m. with the one he'd paid triple for his lawyer to draw up in the middle of the night.

He knew if he hadn't done it she'd have rejected him, his furniture and his job—even if it meant having no money, no place to go—and he wasn't any good at lying. He'd barely been able to look her in the face as he'd fed her all those half-truths this morning.

'I'm here! You ready to go?'

Sylvie sounded like a girl given her first credit card, ready to head to the mall; she couldn't hide her excitement.

'Coming!' he called, and left his room taking the stairs two at a time.

He nearly tripped down five at once when he saw her.

He dated women who dressed in expensive silks, who tossed on jewels worth thousands, wore four-inch heels and glossy chignons that came of spending hours in a salon.

Sylvie wore a green floral print cotton dress with spaghetti straps, old brown sandals with heels maybe two inches high. Her hair was loose, the shine in her curls from simple generic shampoo. She'd probably bought her watch and hoop earrings for ten dollars at the markets. Her face was almost free of cosmetics, but her eyes were enormous with the application of mascara, and her lips shone with pale pink gloss. Her freckles glowed in her pale skin and rosy cheeks. But when she smiled at him like that, so excited to be going *shopping*, he felt fifteen again—gauche as a kid on a date with the girl he'd been moping over for months, hoping for his first kiss. He felt tongue-tied and scared and dizzy—and *scared*.

'Mark? Are you okay?'

He shook himself. 'Sorry. I spaced out for a minute.' He loped down the rest of the stairs. 'I'm ready. Let's go out the back way.'

She snuggled into leather seating with a luxurious sigh. 'Oh…this is so nice. It beats the bus and the train any day.'

He glanced sideways at her. 'You've never owned a car?'

She lifted a brow at him as if he was crazy. 'Duh. Of course I haven't.'

He didn't know what he could say to that—he knew what he wanted to say would be wrong. *Let me buy you a car.*

He could hand her a cheque for the ten

thousand dollars—a number he'd plucked out of the air this morning—but she wouldn't buy a car; and if he bought her one she'd probably sell it, pay her debts and buy presents for everyone. It was her way. Three calls to her brothers today had confirmed his suspicions: her brothers had everything they needed. The family debts hadn't been paid with *their* trust funds.

They'd been shocked by what their sister had done for them. And they'd agreed to keep silence over his plans.

As he pulled out of the garage, he said, 'I haven't caught a bus or a train since before I graduated from uni.'

Her brows lifted. 'Since you were twenty-one?'

'I graduated at twenty-two,' he replied. 'But after I invented the Howlcat air filtration system at nineteen I could actually afford a car.' He grinned at her, hoping she wouldn't ask why he'd been a year behind. When and why he'd fallen a year behind…the stupid mistakes he'd made after Chloe's death.

Mistakes? What he'd done had almost taken a child's life.

Knowing it had happened was bad enough. Talking about it made it worse. What he'd done—the *stupid* decisions he'd made—the drinking and still more drinking when driving—was his private shame, the reason why he'd never have a serious relationship—why this…*wonderful* thing with Sylvie would never go anywhere. That year, his time in rehab and his marriage, were the only things he'd managed to keep from the press. And he had to keep it that way. It could destroy his family and any woman associated with him. And to have Sylvie in his life, his heart and bed, only to lose her—

'Did you go for the obvious and get a convertible?'

Relieved by the teasing note in her voice, he laughed. 'I was a teenage guy who suddenly had more money than he knew what to do with. What do you reckon?'

'I reckon you paid off all the debts for your family, bought them houses and stuff, then helped my family. You took care of everyone else first,' she said softly. 'I reckon you kept living with your parents until everyone was secure—and I reckon you caught a few buses and trains until then, or bought a cheap car first.'

He started at her perception. '*That* didn't make the tabloids. I'm sure of it.'

'I know you—remember?' She laughed, long and gentle, touched with as much affection as amusement. 'You *are* a family man, Mark, first and last. I always knew that. If you hadn't looked after them first, you wouldn't have thought of my family next.'

'You never believed the Heart of Ice stories? You never thought I might have changed with the money?' He gripped the wheel hard, wishing he could work out *what* he thought at this point. She had a way of turning him upside down and inside out without even trying.

'If you had, you wouldn't have remembered us—looked after the boys, as well.' Her voice was so tender it brought a lump to his throat. 'I always knew the person you are, Mark. You could never change to that degree.'

'I'm no saint.' He kept his voice light, hiding the inner darkness. 'A lot of those stories were true.'

Her silence hurt—but when she spoke it wasn't what he expected. 'We all do things we're not proud of to get through a day, to make it to another day, to keep body and soul and family together, to forget what's killing us inside. It doesn't mean we are what others paint us. It only makes us human.'

Her voice held the darkness he'd tried so hard to keep from her—because he couldn't stand to taint her sweet sunshine, to sully her innocence. But she understood desperation—hers to stay alive, to keep her family; his to forget.

Without thinking about their respective positions, he reached out to her, took a clenched hand from her lap and held it. 'At least you had a noble purpose, Sylvie. You can't have done anything to be ashamed of.'

'Don't be so certain.' She frowned out the window. 'Even little china dolls have to live, Mark. Appearances deceive—and once you've sold your soul to survive, you can't have it back. You know that.'

Then, in one of her lightning turnarounds, she pulled her hand from his and gave him a brilliant, glittering smile, thin as spun glass and just as brittle. 'How did we turn from Thrilled to be Shopping Street down Morbid Discussion Road? Let's get back on course. Any type of furniture you absolutely despise?'

'Minimalist,' he replied, wishing he'd made his millions before she'd done whatever it was that had filled her with such self-hate. He was burning with curiosity over what it was she'd done, but seeing the look in her eyes, hearing the repressed self-reproach in her voice, he knew he wouldn't ask. He knew what it was to want to outrun the pain, to leave it all behind, but he also knew it would forever haunt, like a murder victim in an unquiet grave.

No wonder she'd changed her name.

'Good—me, too,' she said with a cheerfulness that was still overdone. 'The cottage is—what?—a hundred years old?'

'About a hundred and thirty. I had it completely revamped when I bought the place, but in its original style. It had been pretty neglected by its former owners.'

'Why didn't you furnish it after that?'

He felt the suspicion lingering beneath the bright tone, and was glad he could tell her the truth. 'I did—I actually had it furnished before I moved into the house. But my first housekeeper had her own furniture and didn't like what I'd put in.'

'Free is good,' she said, with such emphasis he laughed and began to relax. 'What was wrong with it?'

He turned to her for a moment as he negotiated the Anzac Cove Bridge and smiled. 'Nothing, according to you. They were my grandparents' things—actually my great-grandparents' stuff that my grandparents inherited and then left to me. Since I moved it into the main house I've slowly given away the newer stuff I bought, and brought in things I've found at antique and maritime auctions. I like the way it all fits in— and I make sure to get matching wood when I buy a new piece.'

'I think your grandparents' things look perfect in the house.' She sighed dreamily. 'It's all oak and walnut and thick glass. It's lovely solid workmanship, too, and it will last. I'm so glad that your housekeeper didn't want it. If I'd inherited it all and found out it was your family heritage I'd be terrified to ruin it.'

She likes antiques.

If he bought her antiques now she'd reject them, but that didn't mean he couldn't buy her some good, solid furniture in antique style—and if he had to tell the store clerk to pretend it was on special offer and make the cost up later who did it hurt?

He hadn't felt so contented and yet so excited in years. To give Sylvie something of the life and things she deserved had given him a buzz all day.

He'd even sung as he'd worked on the applications to his latest Howlcat design—something he hadn't done for so long he could barely remember. She was his friend, and—

Liar.

Okay, so he wanted her. So he'd almost swerved into oncoming traffic twice because he couldn't keep his eyes off her. His hands were itching to touch her silky skin, to kiss her and take in the sunshine and starlight happiness that flooded his entire being.

But while desire didn't last, the friendship they'd forged felt like his grandparents' furniture…built to last. She was as wholesome as the daisy he'd compared her to, as warm as firelight—and occasionally she burned him, both physically and emotionally, when he came too close. But that was what friends did. She was on a pit-stop in life, on the way to the career and home of her own she deserved, to the man and the family she—

'Mark? Are you all right?' Sylvie broke into his thoughts, lighting up his cold inner darkness with that sunshine voice.

He started and turned to smile at her. 'Sure. Why?'

'You're gripping the wheel so tight.'

He softened his grip, cursing the body language that called him on his delusions. Looking at her, hearing her say his name and feeling high on the cologne-and-pixie-woman smell, even thinking of another man touching her set off something cold, *primal* in him—made him want to pull the car over, haul her into his arms and kiss her into—

Stop it. Think of Sylvie!

He was nowhere near good enough for a woman like her. He didn't have enough of a heart left to give. But he could give her the best home she'd accept, dancing lessons and a friendship that hadn't faded in two decades and wouldn't fade in another ten. One day she'd bring her kids to visit—

'Mark?' She sounded really concerned. 'Mark, are you sure you're okay to drive?'

He frowned at her. 'Of course. Why?'

She pointed to the road ahead. 'You're in two lanes at once.'

Honking horns behind him put him in automatic rescue mode. He moved into the slow lane, and indignant drivers honked again as they passed.

In another few minutes he'd turned into the

parking area of the furniture giant, and showed his invitation card to the parking attendant. He parked, and moved around the car to hand her out—normal practice for him. But she was already out, dancing from foot to foot in an excitement she couldn't hide. The thin veneer of the pretence of helping him choose furniture had been enough excuse for her to blind herself to the truth of his offer—because she'd lived with hand-me-downs and charity store furniture all her life.

He tucked her hand in his, determined to make this a fun-filled night she wouldn't forget—and her infectious, sparkling happiness soaked through their connected skin and streaked through his veins to his heart.

Not to mention other parts he wished would leave him alone. Head, heart and body—all entwined for the first time in half a lifetime. And because she was so *lovable* he couldn't shield himself with his usual wall of ice without her taking it on herself and hurting.

'Hey, Mark, wake up! Are we going?' she demanded, her eyes bubbling with joy like champagne.

Her sweet mirth went straight to his head.

'Come on, let's go.' Smiling with a crazy happiness that even though she was his employee she treated him as she would any other man, he swung her around and, their hands still linked, walked her through the car park.

Once they reached the outside of the megastore he released her hand in case he was recognised. He didn't want Sylvie embroiled in a tabloid situation any more than he thought she'd want to be famous—or infamous.

Uh-oh. This was bad, very bad, if simply unlinking hands made him feel so empty. What was it about Sylvie that made him feel everything twice as much?

Sylvie didn't look at him or comment on it, just kept walking beside him, singing softly in a sweet, slightly tinny voice—and it was all he could do to restrain himself from staring at her. She took his rejection with a respect no woman had ever shown before.

'So, where will we start?' she asked, as if nothing had happened…and maybe from her point of view it hadn't.

'Living, dining, bedroom, white goods—take your pick. I don't know much about furniture, so this is your show,' he replied, waving his hand around the entire place.

'Oh, *oh!*' she cried, veering off to the left.

Grinning, he followed in her wake.

That was how it was for the next hour: she chose, and he and the bemused saleswoman followed her in mingled amusement and admiration.

She promptly fell in love with a fat, comfy, old-fashioned brocade-style sofa, striped like the weird pants she loved, but far more pretty. 'How much is this?'

Mark didn't reach the saleswoman in time, and the woman told her.

Sylvie sighed and shook her head. 'I can't afford that much.' She didn't even look at Mark. She must have worked out a budget and she was sticking to it—even with his money.

Mark nodded meaningfully at the saleswoman. The woman hurried to say, 'Oh, silly me! I was quoting the pre-sale price. Of course it's forty-five percent off.'

Sylvie's piquant face lit and glowed. 'Is it? Oh, yes, I can afford it, then! Mark, I can afford it,' she cried, turning that megawatt smile of happiness on him.

'That's great.' Mark kept his sigh of relief to himself—and his other reactions.

Next she found a small round oak dining table and padded chairs that were within her range without discount, but she still bargained them down a bit. She did the same with a coffee table and with the desk and study chair Mark insisted on, saying housekeepers needed a place to plan the next week's work and menus.

She chose a solid antique-style dressing table, and bedside tables with lamps that would match her old wardrobe. She chose stuff somewhere between average and expensive, but always whittled the saleswoman down to the lowest price she could get.

The woman dropped as low as she could. When Sylvie danced ahead to the next section, the saleswoman whispered, 'I could be fired for this.'

'You won't lose a cent,' he murmured, and she beamed at him. 'I'll pay the right price for anything she wants, but it's all contingent on absolute discretion—both with her and with anyone else.'

'Of course, Mr Hannaford.'

He waved her on to where Sylvie was staring wide-eyed at the latest style of TVs, DVD players and cabinets to hold both. She accepted the woman's explanation that there were special prices for invited customers tonight, and that there was on extra forty to fifty percent off almost everything in her price range.

She picked small things that would suit the cottage, and bargained everything she chose down to the lowest dollar possible. Sylvie was a natural bargainer, used to saving what pennies she could. It didn't matter a bit to her that he had millions and millions of pennies; she was so adorably proud of her bargains he'd never tell her the truth.

She surprised him with her choice of bed. He'd somehow thought she'd choose a four-poster or a white-painted princess-style, but she chose a solid double mattress and base, and bargained for and received free pillows and sheets, a quilt and a cover.

'Thank you for everything, Mr Hannaford. I really appreciate your thoughtfulness at coming with me to fulfil the contract,' she said earnestly, shaking his hand after he put his wallet away. 'The housekeeper's cottage will be perfect now.'

He blanked out for a second before he realised: of course she had to protect herself in front of the saleswoman. A man of his reputation, buying a house full of furniture for a woman could bring unwanted attention on her. His admiration at her cleverness mingled with strong disappointment that she needed to protect herself. That she thought of him that way instead of as a friend—she'd obviously forgotten she'd called him by name earlier.

But he played along, shaking her hand. 'You're welcome, Sylvie. I'm sorry I left it so late. The furniture should have been in the cottage ready when you started work.'

He arranged for delivery and installation with a heavy feeling in his gut. But how could he blame her? It was her integrity even more than her delicate, pretty face that made her so—

Irresistible. It was the only word for her—and with the admission he knew he was in trouble. He'd known the danger from the first minute—seen it from the moment she'd walked into his office that first day and he'd caught his breath at her freckled, pretty face and auburn curls.

Right from the first handshake, he'd known he was in trouble. For the first time, he'd touched a woman and didn't *ache* with a loss so unending he reached out in blind desperation, taking them to a hotel in the need to feel something, anything…

But when he touched Sylvie his whole body smiled. A stupid analogy, but that was how it felt to him. He felt the old feeling take over—one he hadn't felt since he'd heard the word *osteosarcoma*: simple everyday happiness.

Funny how people said that. Strange how people took for granted the fact that they could walk into their house at night, call for the person who belonged to them and they'd be there. They could walk into those arms and give a pecking kiss and say *How was your day?* without ever thinking it could end. Funny how damn *terrifying* it was to begin to believe he could have it.

At least he wasn't beginning to believe he deserved it.

CHAPTER EIGHT

'So now I know what paella tastes like,' Sylvie said on a sigh, taking another forkful. 'My stomach hurts, but I can't stop eating. It's wonderful.'

Mark grinned. 'It's worth the forty-five minute wait for it to come fresh to you. I still love paella, but I branch out now when I come here, and try new items on the menu.'

She nodded with undimmed enthusiasm, not looking at the rabbit concoction he was eating. She'd never been allowed to have a pet—it was a cost they hadn't been able to afford—but the rabbit reminded her of her best friend Scott's pet, Big Ears. She'd loved him so much when she was twelve.

'This place is so…wonderful,' she finished on a lame note, switching from *'romantic'* in a heart-beat, in case he thought she was thinking…

What she *was* thinking. What she wanted so

much her pulse pounded until she could feel it all over her body. She had ever since that kiss on *Harbour Girl*.

'I've been coming here for ten years and I still love it. The atmosphere's amazing—it feels authentic. The owners came from Castile thirty years ago and opened it. I come here when I want authentic Spanish cooking and a private atmosphere.'

He spoke as normal. The soft candlelight, the exotic scent and scene wasn't putting sensuous thoughts in *his* head, obviously. But then why would it when he was used to dating such beautiful women and was only here from obligation and perhaps pity?

So stop thinking about it. Stop wishing for the moon....

She had more than she'd dreamed of even a month ago: a dream job, a wonderful boss, and a growing friendship that blended past and present so seamlessly it was as if they'd always been friends. So why did she keep wishing, hoping?

Poor little Cinderella still wanted her prince to see her, to give her that perfect midnight kiss, to give her a happily-ever-after…

She watched his face in the warm, flickering

light, smiling at her, and she caught her breath, knew she was blushing.

Seeming oblivious to her aching desire for him to touch her, he dipped his fork into the edge of her paella, closing his eyes in culinary rapture as he ate. 'Mmm…I never tire of the flavour.'

An ordinary act, but sharing plates seemed so intimate—and it emboldened her. Carefully avoiding the remains of the rabbit, she tried the spiced potatoes on his plate, and groaned with pleasure as the taste exploded on her tongue. 'Oh….oh, that's *superb*.' And if part of her pleasure was the intimacy of the moment, she never needed to tell him.

The waiter came to refill their glasses, but as before Mark covered his, claiming he was fine with water as he was driving. He nodded at Sylvie's glass. The waiter filled it with Castilian red.

Needing an excuse for her flushed cheeks, she sipped at it. 'Am I very pink? Drinking wine always makes me hot…'

She wanted to sink through the floor when he looked up, an arrested expression in his eyes, and lurking amusement.

'Oh…oh! I meant *physically* hot—not that I

become sexier…um. *Oh.*' Somebody please call the fire brigade! Her face was on fire by this time. 'I think I'll stop talking now,' she whispered in agony. 'This is why I don't like to drink.'

His voice sounded rougher, colder than normal as he said, 'Say what you like. I won't take it the wrong way. I told you—I don't seduce employees.'

Thunk. So that was the sound of your heart hitting your feet… Suddenly the gentleness of all his kisses made horrible sense. He didn't want her; he was trying to *heal* her.

'You've been so kind to me, and I repay you by embarrassing you,' she whispered, her throat tight and her breathing constricted. 'Maybe we should forget dancing and go home. You've given me more than enough for one day.'

'How do you *do* it?' he demanded, his tone as strangled as hers. 'Every single time I act like a jerk, you make me feel even more of one.'

She squirmed in her seat, on the edge of foolish tears. 'I'm sorry—I'm sorry.'

'No, I'm sorry, Sylvie. I'm ruining your nice night.' His voice was warm again. She looked up in anguish and hope, and almost melted when she saw his smile lighting those golden-brown eyes in the firelight, his hair like streaky gold. 'Come on, let's dance.'

He stood and held his hand out to her. Lost in his swift turnaround, mesmerised by him in any mode, she put her hand in his.

A thrill ran through her like quicksilver— intense, almost painful. He was so *wonderful*, and the night, warm and shadowed in this redbrick Castilian cellar, with soft classical guitar music playing, was the stuff of dreams. It wasn't lessened by her plain dress and sandals, his jeans and shirt. They could be wearing sacks or the rags of a fairytale for all she cared or noticed. All she saw was him….

On the floor, he drew her into his arms, and showed her by example how to Salsa. He didn't speak of *dance space* or tell her to straighten her back. He held her and smiled at her, pulled her close and flung her away in Latin-American style. Sylvie felt the drama and excitement of the dance. She revelled in the hot pounding beat of the music, of her blood, loving being so close to him, aching to kiss him one more time—this time to kiss him thoroughly, woman to man.

Did she dare to tell him how she felt?

The music faded out, and a laughing voice

sounded around the room. 'All you lovers out there, you have come on the perfect night. Tonight we want to teach all the women the Jaleo—a Romany dance of love and passion, guaranteed to make your man your slave!'

'Oh…oh,' she breathed. A *free* lesson in sensuous dancing…and Mark would see her dance. Her eyes wide, her heart pounding, Sylvie took a half-step.

'We should go. It's getting late.'

The abruptness of his words dashed cold water on her dreams, her budding courage; she turned her back on the stage and the dance he didn't want her to do for him.

'All right,' she said quietly.

It wasn't as if they were lovers, after all. It wasn't as if they were truly anything but boss and employee with a weird and painful history.

He frowned down at her, and she knew the intensity of her disappointment must be showing in her eyes. 'It's late, and we both have a lot to do tomorrow. I arranged for delivery of your furniture and the installation of the TV and DVD all at once. They'll come soon after five, so you need to be there to tell them where you want everything.'

Sylvie's heart, already splintering from the rejection he'd given without putting it into exact words, dropped to the floor and shattered in silence. 'It doesn't give me much time to remove what I already have, does it?' Her face was white and her head high, jaw tight. 'But you knew it wasn't necessary, didn't you? Because you've been inside.'

He stilled completely. 'We'll talk at home.' He stalked over to the table, threw some bills down, waved at his friends and left the restaurant with a promise to be back soon.

He didn't speak as he handed her into the car, driving straight to Balmain and the house. Sylvie sat huddled in the seat, wanting to shiver in the warmth of the late summer night. What a *sap* she'd been to believe his lies....

He'd been looking after her for years, and he was doing the same now.

She hopped out of the car before he could touch her again and headed for the cottage, more than ready to be alone and cry out her humiliation in peace.

'Would you come in, please? We need to talk.'

'I'd rather not,' she replied, tight and hard.

'I'm not leaving you to think the worst of me. Come inside, please.'

His voice was still taut. She turned on her heel and headed for the house.

It was only when they were inside and safe from prying eyes that Mark softened. He sounded diffident as he picked his way over the shards of her independence. 'I know it must hurt your pride to take what you see as charity, but it isn't. I did give furniture to my first housekeeper—and it has been standard in my contracts with live-in housekeepers.'

'Was the contract I read this morning my original contract, or did you sneak in the cottage—*my home*—to replace it while I slept?' she demanded.

He sighed. 'It should have been in the original. I don't know why my lawyer neglected the clause this time.'

'But he did—you did—until you invaded my privacy and felt sorry for me.' She turned on him in a flash. 'Yes, I'm poor. I have nothing but a lumpy mattress and a rug. But I have my pride, my integrity. I kept that throughout the years when I lost everything else. You can't trample on my pride and then soothe it with your money! *I don't want it*,' she yelled, losing it as hot tears pricked at her eyes, filled and fell. To her surprise, she saw she was barefoot. She'd kicked off her sandals some time during the argument, and now she couldn't see them. 'Where are my sandals?' She had to get out of here before he hurt her more with his charity.

'Hypocrite.'

She gasped and whirled back to face him at the single cool word. 'What?'

He lifted a brow and said, still cool and in control, 'I said you're a hypocrite. So I trampled on your pride and independence?'

Confused, she nodded.

'Tell me how I did that.' He folded his arms and looked down at her from his full six feet to her five-one.

She blinked. 'You know how—with your false contracts and your furniture, splashing your money at me.'

'Right.' He took a step closer, and it was all she could do not to move back. 'I offended your pride by buying you a few pieces of furniture?'

'And by going into my home, my private place, and seeing what I didn't have. What did you do? Make a list of everything I needed?'

'Did *you*?' he shot back, taking another step.

Her hand gripped the arm of the sofa. 'Wh-what?'

He moved right in front of her, so close she could feel the heat of his anger coming from his skin. 'Did you make a list?' he asked with icy precision. 'That first day when you came into my house, did you check my cupboards, my windowsills and my walls and see what I didn't have, make a list of the things you thought I needed?'

She frowned. 'Of course—it's my job…' She faltered, remembering all the things she'd done that weren't in her job description.

'It's your job to clean my house and make breakfast. Anything else is optional and has been from day one.' He went on remorselessly. 'You bought things for me—things you felt my home was missing, the food you found out I liked but didn't have at the time, yes?'

Her eyes widened. 'Well…yes…'

'Did you intend to give me the receipts so I could reimburse you, since you haven't touched the grocery money I left for you?'

Her toe began scuffing on the living room rug. 'They were *gifts*, Mark.'

'As were mine to you—but whereas I accepted graciously—' he ignored her as she snorted, remembering his 2:00 a.m. wake-up call '—I knew you wouldn't.'

'I spent a measly hundred or two!' she cried. Well, four hundred. But she wasn't going to tell him that, either.

'How much do you have in the bank, Sylvie?'

The furious demand left her sinking deeper in the mire of confusion. 'Why would you want to know—?'

'How much do you have left after buying those gifts for me?' he repeated, with a quiet cold control that enraged her over again.

'One hundred and forty-seven dollars and something cents,' she shouted. 'Happy now? Knowing how far apart we are?'

'This isn't about who has what,' he said quietly. 'It's about why you feel you can give to me, but why it's *offensive* for me to give to you. Why it's okay for you to break the contract by making dinners, spending almost everything you have on decorating my house and buying me food I like, but you find it *offensive* for me to spend a far lower percentage of what I have on your happiness because I consider you a friend. You're allowed to care about me and give to me, but you won't allow me the same joy of giving because you have pride?'

Put like that, there was nothing to say… But…

'I wanted you to be *happy*,' she cried wretchedly.

'Well, I was happy today—until you threw it in my face. I thought we were more than boss and employee, Sylvie. I thought we were friends—both all those years ago and now.'

'We are,' she cried. 'But—but it's always been you giving to me.'

'Has it?' He reached out and took her hands in his. 'Leaving money aside, which isn't the most important thing a person can give, has it *always* been me doing the giving?'

His touch soothed and aroused her at the same time, put her mind in a whirl—forcing her to think harder. 'A wet flannel, a few hugs…some food. That's all.'

'A friend who sat with me when I was so alone and scared I could scream. An overburdened girl who stayed beside me and gave me a hug when no one else saw how badly I needed it. A child who showed me how to make and keep a promise even if it hurt.' He released her hands to cup her face in his palms. His beautiful eyes looked so deeply into hers she wanted to cry all over again. 'A woman who came back into my life, saw through my façade and told it like it is—who won't let me eat or live alone…who tells me off, risks her job for my sake. You forced me out of hiding, Sylvie. The things you want from me are for me. They have nothing to do with my money or fame.' He drew her into his arms and held her with a gentle affection that made the lump in her throat unbearable. 'Any rich person can throw money at a problem—but the gifts you give are far more priceless than money. Don't despise them, Sylvie.'

With a few simple sentences he'd done more than show her what she meant to him—he'd given her pride back, so precious to her. Giving in to her own need, she wrapped her arms around his waist, her cheek against his heart. 'You didn't keep your promise to her,' she whispered.

'I know.' He laid his chin on her hair. He didn't explain; he didn't have to.

'She'd be so sad, seeing you like this.'

He shook his head, messing her curls. 'Not like this, not tonight. She'd be glad you came back into my life. I've been alone too long, lived too many years without the kind of friendship we have.' He hesitated; she could feel the indecision in him before he said it. 'I don't want to break that friendship, Sylvie. I don't want you to feel pressured to leave your position. One day, when it's time for you to move on, just tell me and we'll still be friends.'

She fought the urge to turn her face, kiss the cotton and skin covering his heart, the loyal heart whose ice only existed because it still hadn't mended, because it still loved a girl long gone. She wanted to dash at the tears slipping down her face, but let them go. 'All right, then, I'll take the stupid furniture. I'll even *like* the stuff. Happy?'

He chuckled and ruffled her hair further with the underside of his chin. 'Yeah.'

'I should go,' she murmured, as the craving to kiss him became intolerable. 'It's late, and I have exams tomorrow. Today,' she amended, as she checked the grandfather clock slowly ticking with its copper pendulum.

'Bring your notes in in the morning and I'll quiz you.'

'Thanks.' The word was husky as she fought against saying the words that would break his sweet delusion that *one day* would ever come and she would move on.

'I'll bring home dinner for us tomorrow. You study when you come home from college.'

Home, he'd said. *For us*. As if there was an 'us'

for them, or as if their shared meals were more than a boss being kind. Her heart soared with hope; her eyes twinkled. 'You really want fish and chips, don't you? Isn't my cooking good enough for you?'

He laughed. 'Most of the time—but this place does the best fish and chips in town.'

'All *right*,' she groaned. 'We'll have a picnic then.'

'Good.' He moved out of her arms, his mouth smiling a little, his eyes intense. 'Goodnight, Sylvie. Sleep well.' He was looking at her mouth—and she caught her breath. She almost believed he wanted to kiss her as much as she ached for it….

But it was too late now. The moment had come and gone on the dance floor.

So she smiled back and waved, as if she hadn't laid her heart all but bare for him to see, and his blinkered eyes had only seen half the truth. 'Thanks. You too.'

She left her discarded sandals somewhere, like Cinderella's glass slipper—but she wore a dress from the markets, her shoes were factory seconds and her beautiful lost prince had already fitted the right shoe to the perfect princess.

She'd find them tomorrow—when she returned to real life, when she was back where she belonged, cooking and cleaning for him.

CHAPTER NINE

WHAT was he *doing*?

He berated himself all the way home, with the scent of fresh fish and chips rising from the paper on the passenger seat making his stomach growl. This was stupid—worse, it was irresponsible. He'd known it from the start. Hadn't he argued with himself before dancing with her that first time?

Touching her had been the mistake of his life— *No, not quite*, he thought wryly, *but it's the third*.

And still he couldn't wait to do it again…

'Well, about time, Hannaford. Talk about keeping a lady waiting. I was going to start the picnic without you.' She waved a near-empty wineglass at him.

She was sitting on the grass in the backyard, with a blanket, a bottle and two glasses when he emerged from the garage. In a simple sundress the colour of autumn leaves with crossover straps, her hair loose and her feet bare, she turned around from contemplating the dancing lights on the harbour at night and smiled at him—she didn't have a scrap of make-up on, and her clean-scrubbed freckled face was just so *adorable*—and every one of his fears and arguments was sucked down a drain called happiness.

'Without the food?' he teased her as he sat down.

She sighed. 'That was the part I couldn't work out.'

He grinned and laid the paper-wrapped food in the centre of the blanket. 'The feast awaits, my lady, with my deepest regrets for keeping you waiting.'

'You're not eating like that—all trussed up in a monkey suit. Up you go.' She picked up the food and carried it inside, putting it in the oven. 'A picnic isn't a picnic until you're barefoot and no fancy threads.'

When he returned in surf shorts and a T-shirt, feet bare, she nodded in beaming approval, said in mock-admiration, 'You look hot,' and handed him a glass.

He threw a brief glance at the bottle: non-alcoholic. And though it meant she knew part of his secret, he relaxed and lifted the glass. 'To howling cats and Ginger wannabes.'

'Done.' She sipped at her drink. 'I'm so glad you prefer non-alcoholic. I become pretty silly after one glass. Could never handle alcohol at all.'

No way was he taking that less-than-subtle opening and telling her the real reason why he never drank. He'd rather she thought him a re-covered alcoholic than knew about Robbie Allsopp, a kid having a good time on his bike until a binge-drunk seventeen-year-old, wild with grief and loss, trying to forget the past, sped around a corner…

So he asked, 'So…you think I look hot?' Teasing her again, inhaling the sweet scent of talcum powder or some similar perfume. 'Did you mean physically, as in from the heat, or dare I hope you no longer consider me downright ugly?'

She gave an exaggerated sigh as she laid the feast open. 'I told you you're good-looking once, Hannaford. Stop fishing for compliments.' She helped herself to food without a plate, and closed her eyes.

'Another hungry person's prayer?' he asked when she began to eat.

She sighed again and rolled her eyes. 'My faith might be simple, but don't knock it because you're an infidel.'

He shook his head and picked up some fish, smearing it with lemon and tartare sauce. 'A big judgement call for someone who's never asked me what I believe.'

'Are we turning theological now?' she complained. 'I'm too hungry to discuss the mysteries of life.' She turned and lay on her tummy on the blanket, her body facing the harbour, her face ecstatic as she ate. 'A clear summer night, wine, ocean views and marvellous food. Where else would you find this luxury?'

He almost laughed, thinking of any of his usual dates' reactions to a barefoot fish-and-chips picnic in his backyard; but then no other woman he'd met was quite like Sylvie, revelling in every experience that came her way. 'No idea.'

'The fish is perfect—not overcooked or soggy. Where did you buy it?'

He was deriving more enjoyment from watching her eat than he was from his own food. 'The fish markets beneath the Anzac Bridge. They batter and fry it while you wait. It's from a fresh catch.'

'Ah.' She nodded. 'Far better than Greasy Joe's down the road from our house. He half-cooks the battered fish and leaves it there for hours until some poor sap gets hungry enough to order it. And don't get me started on the potato scallops.' She shuddered.

'Is it really called Greasy Joe's?' he asked, since that was an Aussie euphemism for most fish and chip/hamburger stores.

She frowned and pursed her mouth. 'Yeah, right,' she snorted. 'How far from your roots have you come, Hannaford? All those five-star restaurants and fancy charity dos have made you forget the important things.'

'Like Greasy Joe's?' he retorted, holding in a grin. 'That's important?'

Her chin on one palm as she ate, she nodded, with an adorable seriousness that made him want to laugh at her. 'It's the little things—like fast food and picnicking in the backyard…tinkering with improvements to go-carts and bike wheels instead of working on things that will sell around the world…having fun in a workshop here instead of the big fancy one with shiny doodads you've no doubt got in Howlcat Industries—they're the things that make life meaningful.

Success and wealth can't make you happy if you forget who you are.'

'And who am I?' he asked coldly.

'A guy who likes fish and chips in the backyard but probably hasn't done it in years,' she said softly. 'A guy who probably remembers the best times of his life as inventing stuff that would never work in the smelly, dusty old workshop his mum and dad let him have.' She looked away, frowning over the harbour, and he knew she was going to say something that would rip out his guts before she said it. 'A guy who held his girl-friend's vomit bowl and changed her sheets and pyjamas because she felt humiliated when the staff did it.'

'How the *hell*—?' Then he stared at her with narrowed eyes. Though not shocked, he was more appalled than he'd expected to be. He scrambled to his feet. 'You talked to her?'

She nodded without apology. 'I used to read to her sometimes, when you were all gone, and we'd talk. Or she would.' With a frown and a sigh she said, 'I think it was a relief to her to talk to me. She didn't have to pretend she wasn't scared with me, or act strong and say it was okay. Sometimes we lashed out, or cried together.

Neither of our lives was fair…what was happening to us.'

Air whooshed from his lungs; he sat down before he fell down. 'She sent you here, didn't she? She foisted one of her impossible promises on you—*a thirteen-year-old kid.*'

Her eyes shimmering with tears, she nodded.

For the first time in many years he felt simmering anger at Chloe. How could she have done that—and to a girl who'd had more than enough burdens to cope with? 'What was it?' he asked with grim foreboding. 'What did she make you promise?'

After a visible hesitation she said it—with a simplicity that told him it was a relief for her to tell him. 'If, by the time I was grown up and free from my obligations, you still hadn't fulfilled your promise to her, she wanted me to come back into your life, and—and be your friend, make you smile again.' She smiled mistily with a love for his dead wife undimmed through the years. 'She said I had a knack for that.'

'In general, or with me?' he asked, unable to let the subject go although he knew they were straying into dangerous waters.

She sighed. 'Both, I guess, since I could always make her smile, too.'

Fury filled him and overflowed, despite knowing Chloe had been right—maybe he was so furious *because* she was right. Gratitude and guilt mingled with the horror of what Chloe had done to Sylvie. 'She had no right to ask it of you. A girl already overburdened!'

'She knew you, didn't she? She knew if you ended up giving your promise you'd be lying.' Her gaze rested on him. In the night lights sending soft light down from the garage roof and the flood of summer moonlight her eyes took on a glow from within, looked darker, like mulled wine through firelight. 'It's not a crime to love someone so much you want them to be happy. I don't think she should have forced you into your promise, and I'm sure she thought I was too young to remember what I said I'd do, or remember you, either, by the time I was grown up. But it eased her fears for you—it made her passing easier.'

'You were only thirteen. It's been fifteen years.'

She shrugged. 'There are some people you just can't forget. Some promises stay with you through the years.'

Mark felt differently, but said nothing. Sylvie had been unlike any kid he'd known, with a compassion and maturity few adults ever achieved. He couldn't imagine anyone but her remembering a promise—even one of this magnitude.

'She was…unforgettable.' He heard the jerking of his voice. Yeah, he was mad at Chloe and she deserved it, but still he missed her.

'So were you,' Sylvie said softly.

He started and stared at her. 'Only because you saw me in the tabloids.'

'That was it in part, and the money you gave us,' she admitted without shame. 'But you underrate yourself,' she went on, in that tender, dreaming voice. 'I was a lonely, romantic kid with too much to do physically, but my mind was free. So I dreamed a lot.' She smiled at him. 'I'd see your picture somewhere and I'd dream of you. You became the prince of my fairytales— and Chloe was the princess. I wanted to be the princess—as girls do—but I never could see myself that way. I was always the one cleaning up after Prince Mark and Princess Chloe. And here I am, still doing it. It's my fate, I tell you,' she said in a mock-melodramatic tone, and laughed.

She didn't sound in the least self-pitying, yet Mark forgot his anger, his feeling of being overwhelmed by the intrusions into his personal life—he forgot about himself altogether. He ached for the overworked child she'd been, dreaming dreams of becoming his *housemaid*— and that was what she'd become. She'd come down from being the princess of fairy stories to being a real maid. Her dreams had narrowed to a life of servitude.

So he was going to make her feel like a princess....

'I have a charity event I need to attend Friday night—' he began, but her laughter had stilled, and she was shaking her head with a frantic kind of determination. 'Why?' he asked, curt with the sting of rejection. 'Surely there's no point in denying this thing between us?'

'Maybe, but not in public. I won't do it.' She jumped to her feet and began scrabbling around to clean up.

He laid a hand on her arm. 'Stop it, Sylvie, and talk to me. Being famous is part of my life, and if you're going to be any part of it—'

'I'm not,' she shot back, so bluntly it took him aback. 'I'm your housekeeper, Mark. *Your employee*. I belong *here*—this is where I stay.'

His eyes narrowed. He needed no clarification

on what she meant. 'Then why did you start something you had no intention of finishing by kissing me? You always knew I had a public profile. It's part of who I am.'

'You kissed me, actually—and we played house for a couple of days. I always knew that was all we'd ever have.' She picked up the paper again. 'This is who *I* am, Mark—the cleaner. What we are is worlds apart.'

With a lightning movement he brought his arms down on the wrappers in her hands, scattering them. 'Don't you *ever* demean yourself that way again,' he snarled, grabbing her hands in his to stop her from bolting—but she didn't struggle, just looked up at him with those big eyes of hers, and he felt a hard thrill run through him. She did trust him, as she'd claimed this morning. 'You're worth so much more than you set yourself!'

The look in her eyes was pure puzzlement as she stared at him. Her chest heaved. 'I'm fine with who and what I am.'

'Are you?' he said, eyes narrowed. 'Then why do you lower what you do? It's *just* home-baked muesli. It's *just* lasagne. I'm *just* the cleaner. You do it all the time. What you are as a person isn't defined by the work you do!'

'Isn't it?' she panted, facing him down, all five-one of her, looking up at him unintimidated. 'It's how the world defines people. *I'm a doctor. I'm a lawyer. I'm an inventor.*' Her jaw tightened as she said again, 'I'm a cleaner.'

'And why is that?' Hands tightening on her arms, but without force, he glared at her. 'Why did you start cleaning in the first place?'

The confusion grew in her eyes. 'You know why. My family…'

'Exactly. You did it to take care of your family. You kept them together. You paid the bills. Your father died in peace at home, and your brothers are all respected professional men because of your sacrifices.'

She was shaking her head before he finished. 'No. That was you. Without the trust funds you set up—'

He had to struggle now to hold on to his anger and allow himself to say what she needed most to hear. 'Your brothers are all highly intelligent men who'd have found a scholarship somewhere. All I did was give them a leg up. It was *you* who saved them. They had time to study and get the marks they did because you did everything for them. From the time your mother became sick—

when you were only *eight*—you began your adulthood. By the time you were thirteen you were already everything to your family: mother, nurse, cheer squad, cook and, yes, cleaner. *You* kept your family together. You gave your brothers a normal life at the expense of your own.'

She closed her eyes. 'It wasn't like that....'

'Wasn't it?' he asked softly, the urge to touch her becoming unbearable. 'Funny, that's what they tell me.'

Her eyes flew open. 'You've seen the boys?'

'I called them all today.'

She stiffened. 'What did you want? What did they say?'

'I didn't ask about *that*, though it was pretty hard holding back,' he said, knowing what she feared most. 'I could tell Simon knew.'

'What did they tell you?'

'Apart from what I just said, you mean?' He shrugged. 'They're your brothers and totally loyal to you. What do you think they said? They said I'd have to hear it from you.'

She relaxed visibly. 'Why?' she whispered, and he knew what she wanted to ask.

'Because you fascinate me. I don't know why you set such low labels on yourself and what you do for others,' he said quietly. 'You won't tell me. I want to know why you break your back trying to make others' lives work for them, and why, though you smile and laugh, there's so much sadness beneath the mask. You'll do anything to make people happy, but you seem to think *you* don't deserve the kind of happiness you give to others. You even brought a lone-wolf inventor out of living a lie with your wisdom and courage, your unfailing optimism in a life that would have made so many people hard and bitter,' he added, wanting to touch her so badly it felt like a fist squeezing his heart.

She shrugged again. 'A few things I bought. Some home-made meals. It's no big deal.'

'You're doing it again—demeaning yourself and what you do,' he said quietly. 'Don't you see that cleaning is the least of what you do, who you are? You're the best friend I've had since she died. You make me look forward to getting up every day. You're so beautiful you make me ache, yet you turn your back on personal happiness, only seeing what you can do for others.' He drank in the warmth of her cheek against his palms, only realising he'd cupped her face after the coldness in him diminished. 'You're a woman of extraordinary strength and compassion, Sylvie Browning,' he murmured as he bent to her. She lifted her face, waiting. 'You're exactly the sort of woman I knew you'd become. That's why I never forgot you. You were amazing at eight, incredible by ten, unforgettable at thirteen, and you're even more amazing now.'

And then, finally, he kissed her.

For a moment she didn't respond. Then with a tiny moan she moved into his arms, kissing him back, warm and sweet as marshmallows toasted over a fire, soft as his garden on a spring night, like daisies when they'd begun to bloom. Even her kiss made him think of sunshine and smiles and laughter. He was addicted to the way she made him feel.

Here in her arms, held in thrall by the ordinary everyday happiness of touching her, he knew the truth: he was falling for her, bungee-jumping at breakneck speed into love with an adorable, wonderful woman who refused to come into his world…and he could no longer go into hers.

'Is what happened to you the reason you won't go public with me?' he murmured against her mouth, and held her against him as she stiffened. 'It's not what's between us—we both know this is too strong to walk away from—and it's not that you're not good enough for me. If anything, it's the other way around. So tell me, Sylvie. I deserve to know.'

He felt the shuddering exhaled breath come from the deepest part of her, felt it against his shirt, warming his skin, and he felt absurd hope.

Then she said softly, 'I can't. I *can't*.'

For a moment the streaking pain of her rejection felt like crash-cart paddles on his chest, stopping his heart. Then, too late, he remembered the reason he *didn't* deserve to know—the reason he had to walk away from this, from her—and he nodded. 'All right.'

She looked up at him. 'All right? Just like that?'

She was so pretty, looking up at him in wonder, as if he'd pulled her from a burning car wreck. Keeping her secret from him meant that much to her—and though it hurt he couldn't make himself do the noble thing and walk away.

And too late he understood why. Though part of him still loved Chloe, there was another person who'd always been snuggled inside his heart. The girl Mary had walked inside his soul years ago, claiming her share of his love by being who she was. As a woman Sylvie had walked back into his life with that same brave, defiant smile, the same courageous outspokenness and unstinting giving, and his ice—had melted. Just like that.

Falling for Sylvie? Nah, he was all the way gone—completely and utterly in love. And though he knew it couldn't last for them, he had some work to do before she left his life. He'd do whatever it took to make her see her worth, to show her what an extraordinary, *wonderful* person she was.

'Yeah, just like that,' he said huskily. 'So, Miss Browning, would you care to dance?'

She blinked, drew in a slow breath; her eyes lit and sparkled. Her hands, still around his neck, drew him down for a long kiss, her fingers caressing his hair. The sparkling joy that was Sylvie wrapped around him and filled him to overflowing.

'Why, yes, Mr Hannaford, I'd be honoured,' she replied when they finally, reluctantly, let go.

Then she shoved the papers from dinner in the recycling bin, shoved the glasses in his hand and snatched up the wine bottle. She took his free hand and led him into the house, put the remnants of their picnic on the counter, and led him on into the ballroom.

Throwing open the wide French doors, she ran

past him with a sweet, naughty smile and put on some music. 'We're shifting gear tonight.'

Rhythmic clapping filled the room; an eighties classic boomed out. Sylvie did a little shimmy and pointed at him. She pulled him to her by his shirt; laughing, he came, and they jumped around. She sang to him in her pretty, slightly tinny voice.

If he'd never forgotten her before, he knew he'd spend the rest of his life regretting the months of stupidity that made him forever unworthy of this strong, beautiful woman who'd overcome the tragedy and drudgery of her past to reach for every particle of happiness she could find and share that shimmering joy in living with him. She'd brought him back to life, taught him to let go of the past, to seek happiness and hold on to it while it was there.

As they danced for the next half-hour to all her favourite songs, he faced the truth: he didn't deserve a woman as *wonderful* as Sylvie, and though it made his guts twist and his heart scream with denial he had to accept it.

So he'd take what he could get with her, heal her of her hurts if he could and then let her go with a smile.

But, dear God in heaven, what would become of him then?

CHAPTER TEN

'So how do I look?'

On the sofa, scribbling down notes for an assignment due next week, Sylvie tossed an angry glance at the stairwell—and lost the ability to speak. In a tux he was breathtaking. She couldn't *breathe*....

She squashed the unreasonable resentment that he was still going—taking one of his usual women. He'd told her this charity event was vital; he'd asked her first. She had no right to be jealous or to wonder if he'd be home tonight.

But she was, and she did.

She gulped down the screaming need to say something to keep him here with her and gave him a smile that felt brittle on her lips. 'Hot, boss. Totally hot. Your date's got no hope of competing.'

He came down the stairs and stood in front of her. 'There's no contest,' he said with soft meaning. 'I needed someone to sit with, Sylvie.'

Her stomach clenched hard; it was all she could do not to press her lips together. 'I know. It's cool.' *Don't ask...don't say it...* 'Cinderella doesn't have a dress to match that tux, boss, and no fairy godmother, either. You're better off with what's-her-name.' She wheeled away from him. 'Anyway, I have a hotter date than yours could ever be,' she announced, with a gaiety that sounded as much of a lie as the smile she'd given him. 'I should head out.'

'What?' He turned her back round, his eyes boring into hers. 'Who is he?'

She stared up at him and panted. 'Have I asked who *your* date is?'

He growled, 'Amie's an old friend in a long-term relationship. She agreed to sit with me because her boyfriend's running this gig. It's the only reason I'm going—to support a friend's pet cause. It's for Medicin Sans Frontiers.'

She almost melted on the spot. 'And my date is an adorable seven-month-old called Nicky Browning. Drew and Shelley need a night out. The baby's just over croup.'

Mark laughed and pulled her up into his arms. 'Have I ever told you you're a brat?' He looked down at her for an intense moment, then he kissed her with a lingering sweetness that *did* make her melt. 'Keep tomorrow free… Oh, and Sunday, as well. Tell your brothers you'll be out of town until Sunday night.'

Delight flooded her. A full weekend with Mark?

Where?

Aiming for a careless tone, she asked, 'Oh? Why and wherefore? And where?'

'It's a secret…but you can stop worrying. It's nothing that puts us in the public eye. In fact, it's very private—and we have separate rooms,' he said softly, and shivers of arousal, disappointment and relief raced through her. 'I'm not asking you, Sylvie, I'm telling you. You're coming with me.'

She had no intention of denying him—or herself. 'I'd bow in submission, my lord, but it's rather difficult at this present moment,' she retorted with a laugh, wiggling against him.

'If you move like that much longer I won't be going anywhere tonight but here with you,' he growled.

She felt a frisson of panic run through her. Immediately he let her down to the floor and released her.

'It's getting better, isn't it—the fear?' he asked softly, smiling down at her.

Startled to realise he was right, she nodded. The fear, a constant companion since she was fifteen, was receding so fast she couldn't see where it had gone. When Mark touched her, she felt not merely cherished and safe…she felt *beautiful*.

'Are you ready? I'll drop you to Drew's on the way.'

Relieved that he didn't probe her when she didn't know what to say—how could she tell him, *I'm only better when the man touching me is you?*—her brow lifted. 'Are you serious? You'll drop me to Ermington on your way to Darling Harbour?'

He grinned. 'Trust you to argue with me even if it saves you a train and a bus ride. It's only fifteen minutes out of the way. Come on.'

'You'll be late.'

He shrugged. 'I'm stag tonight anyway, so who'll care?'

A vision flashed into her brain: a stunningly attired Mark making a late entrance, all the single women taking note that he was alone…

She almost said she'd change and go with him, or told him to forget going away for the weekend. Pride and jealousy were a self-destructive combination—one she never knew she'd feel for any man—but this wasn't any man; this was Mark. After swallowing the hard ball in her throat, she summoned up a bright false smile. 'Let's go, then.'

And while he did his thing—out in a tux with all the beautiful people—she did what she did best: cooked and cleaned and changed dirty nappies…and wondered when he'd be home.

When she came home, after eleven-thirty, the big house was in darkness. And though she knew it was stupid she sat in the cottage, studying again—or trying to—knowing she was waiting for a light to come on.

It was almost one before the lights came on in the garage, and she felt pure bliss flooding her soul. He didn't bring women home. Rita, his mother, had assured her of that. And though it was ridiculous, she had the sense that he'd come home to *her*.

She switched off her lights before he saw a foolish, needy woman waiting for her man to come home…because he wasn't and never could be hers for long.

'Oh. *Oh*,' she breathed, at Mark's latest surprise of the morning.

He'd already made breakfast for her: her favourite Sunday pancakes but on a Saturday, with strawberries and maple syrup and fresh coffee. And now he wouldn't let her clean the mess, but said he'd hired a cleaning woman for the day.

'And don't pack a thing—you won't need it,' he said with a mysterious air. 'This weekend you don't do a thing but enjoy yourself.'

Her brows lifted in wonder, but the gentleness in his eyes, the acceptance that she was far from ready for the next step in a strange half-relationship with too many secrets, helped her trust in him to overcome the panic. She felt absurdly shy as she nodded.

'Good. Now, take this.' He held out a long embossed box to her, with the name of a famous designer on it.

She gasped and took it, her fingers trembling. She retreated to the cottage for a few minutes, and came out wearing a deceptively simple dress. It was pure linen, a soft leaf-green, with a light autumn-coloured jacket. There was also a pair of matching sandals, by a label she'd only dared peek at in store windows now and then, for they cost a month's mortgage payments. She came back to the house, intensely shy and a little proud of herself—and a woman was waiting with a mobile hairdressing unit. She washed and treated Sylvie's hair, and dried it so the curls bounced and shone.

'You have such lovely natural highlights in your hair I don't need to add any—and I'd rather leave it curling like this,' the woman said, smiling at Sylvie. 'You have hair women pay hundreds for.'

She'd never thought of her hair that way before. She flicked a glance at Mark, who was working on some kind of drawing design at his desk. He turned and smiled at her, nodding in agreement. 'I love her hair as it is,' was all he said, and her insides turned to jelly.

After the woman was gone he smiled again, a more intimate, private look in his eyes. 'You look beautiful.'

Then he led her out—not the back way to the car, but to the front door...

She blinked hard, winking away the silly tears forming in her eyes, and turned to him, feeling the radiance shining from her pores. 'This day has been—been...'

He touched her face with an expression approaching tenderness. 'This is just the start.' He opened the door of a big white stretch limousine with a flourishing bow. 'My lady.'

As if she truly was a lady he handed her

inside—and she saw the champagne glasses, the bottle and the crushed strawberries.

'It's non-alcoholic, of course,' he said as he slid in beside her. 'As we both prefer.' His eyes twinkled.

Unable to hold back anymore, she cupped his face in her hands and kissed him, soaking herself in the joy of being in his arms as he drew her closer with a soft groan. With no words to say how she felt, she let her lips speak to him in silence.

When they finally parted, he whispered, 'You're welcome.' He reached for the strawberries and filled the base of the glasses.

By the time she'd finished her first strawberry champagne in a limousine, the driver had pulled up at Kingsford-Smith Airport.

With her mouth falling open, she turned to Mark. 'Um, where are we going? I don't have a passport....'

He leaned over and whispered in her ear, 'Ever heard of Turtle Island?'

Her eyes wide, she shook her head. 'Is that in the Great Barrier Reef?'

He kissed the ear he spoke into. 'It certainly is. It's the most exclusive island in the chain north of Cairns. It's where people go when they don't want gossip or the press.'

Touched to the deepest part of her heart by his thoughtfulness—and at this weekend that must be taking a massive bite out of even such a rich man's wallet—she laid her head on his shoulder. 'I don't know what to say.'

'What you said before, and the way you said it, was pretty well perfect,' he replied, alluding to her kiss with a teasing tone. 'But we should wait until we're on the jet.'

She blinked. 'We're going on a jet?'

His brows lifted. 'I promised you privacy. Big-name journalists quite often get paid first- or business-class flights to their assignments—and while they may not care what I do and who with, they might pass on the info to a contact with lower journalistic principles.'

He'd thought of everything.

Feeling like a true VIP, she enjoyed being ushered through an area reserved only for those taking private charters. Mark generously tipped those who expedited their travel. Then they were on a small jet, with wide seats and luxurious appointments.

Sylvie clung tight to Mark's hand all the way through her first take-off, squealing with the losing-her-tummy feeling. 'The boys and I went to Australia's Wonderland once, with the people from Stewart House, and the Bush Beast felt just like that!'

She could have bitten out her tongue at the thoughtless words. *Stewart House?* Why didn't she just take a permanent marker and write *'charity child'* on her forehead? They'd only ever asked for help once, when she'd become too sick to care for the family, and a neighbour, concerned, had called the famous charity. For a year they'd offered housekeeping help, free trips to the doctor for her father and fun outings for all four kids.

Her father had tried to call an end to it after that year, saying there must be thousands of people who truly needed help and they didn't. For once Sylvie, only fourteen at the time, had bucked against him, saying *she* didn't need the help, but the boys needed it. Drew and Simon in particular were doing nothing but work and study, and would have rebelled if those treats had been taken away from them.

Dad had been in a wheelchair by then, with the scleroderma that would eventually take his life, helpless against her angry demand. He'd capitulated with a bitterness that still rang in her heart. *'If you're willing to lower yourself enough to take charity, I'm not!'*

After a pregnant silence Mark said, 'So, I remember mentioning the way you speak to me the best...?'

He drew her into his arms, and as they kissed the churning confusion in her heart became lost in the haunting beauty of his touch, in the joy of all he'd done to make this weekend perfection.

The only question was: what could she ever give him in return?

'So, which of the dresses would you like to wear tonight?' asked the beaming saleswoman at the resort boutique.

Still unable to believe this was her life, even if only for a day or two, Sylvie said, 'Which do you think, Beverley?'

Beverley's smile grew even wider, more maternal, though she was barely forty. 'I definitely think the ivory-gold. Soft autumn tones bring out the highlights in your hair and make your eyes look incredible. And we have the perfect shoes—some gorgeous russet two-inch-heeled courts—' She shook her finger as Sylvie tried to turn down the offer. 'Mr Hannaford was very specific. *"Spoil her completely,"* were his exact words. *"Show her everything, give her anything she wants."'*

If she hadn't already been totally crazy about the man, those words would have done it. All her life she'd dreamed of one fairytale night, and he was giving it to her… 'I know—he would say that. But—'

Beverley interrupted, laughing. 'But nothing. This is my weekly quota you're denying! Just look at the shoes before you say another word, okay?'

She was vacillating already, and Beverley's quota comment had weakened her; she allowed the saleswoman to bring out 'a few' boxes. And once she saw the russet shoes she was as big a sucker as any other woman. *Shoes…beautiful shoes.* Six pairs of them, one for each of her new outfits.

And then came the stunning jewellery, the exquisitely light make-up…

That night, when Mark knocked on the door of her deceptively simple beachfront cabin, she was in the shimmering ivory-gold silk dress and the russet shoes, make-up on, simple ruby studs in her ears and a pendant around her neck—she'd refused even to consider the diamonds.

'You're beautiful,' he said simply when she opened the door to him. He held out a single amber rose with a deep golden heart, matching the colours she liked best.

He'd noticed.

The moonlight on the soft-lapping waves framed him like a halo. She caught her breath, wondering anew that this was her life even for a day; that this man—this incredible, giving man could want her. The glow in her heart had to be reflected on her face.

'Thank you.' He was more beautiful than she could ever be—with or without the classic tuxedo he wore.

'What, no comments about me being hot?' He tipped up her face, smiling with his eyes, as well as his mouth. Smiling with his heart.

'You said the words I wanted to. You're a word thief, Hannaford,' she murmured, wrinkling her nose at him in an effort to be playful when all she wanted was—

'Then I take them back.' As she glared at him in indignation, he added, 'You look perfect. Well, almost perfect.' He pulled a handkerchief and dusted it over her nose and cheeks, removing the covering powder. 'I like your freckles.'

She had to close her mouth somehow or she'd blurt it out. *I love you.* No way would she put *that* burden on him. He was fond of her; he wanted to help her; he desired her—and that was enough of a miracle in itself. His love belonged to Chloe. If that hadn't changed in all these years he wasn't going to fall for someone like her.

There you go, demeaning yourself again. But if he knew her secret he wouldn't look at her as if she was wonderful to him. He'd leave her life at a million miles a minute.

The time was coming; she knew she couldn't stop it. Keeping her secret had begun to feel as if she was lying to him. Something died inside her every time he was so gentle and compassionate when she didn't deserve it. So she'd take all the joy she could with him, then tell him the truth and leave with only the same regrets she'd had when she came.

'I want to kiss you,' she whispered, as intense as a summer day before storm.

'Then do it. Kiss me, Sylvie.' He came into the room, closed the door behind him and stood before her, giving her choice and power.

She only hesitated for a moment. Then she moved her hands to his shoulders and up, winding her fingers through his hair. She breathed in his scent, felt the heat and need in his skin, and the now-familiar pulse of excitement and desire took over. 'Mark, oh, *Mark*…' She lifted up on her toes, brought him down to her and kissed him.

When he stayed still, using only his mouth to arouse her, she gave an impatient moan and put his hands on her waist, coming closer, deepening the kiss. Moving against his hard, ready body only made her crave more of him. Her hands grew feverish, needing to touch him, all of him; her lips wandered down his throat. She was aching to open his shirt and press her lips to his heated skin. She pulled at his tie.

He put his hand over hers. 'Sylvie.' The way he said her name—so gravelly with rough desire— sent hurtling thrills though her. 'You know where this is heading?'

'Yes, yes…' She drew him down for another kiss. 'I need you, Mark. I'm aching, burning inside. I need to touch you, to kiss your skin. I want you now…'

He groaned and kissed her, his hands moving over her through the silky dress until she writhed against him, making soft noises of feminine arousal; he slowed the pace, nuzzling her mouth and whispering between brushing kisses: 'Tonight, sweetheart, if you're still ready, we'll make love all night.'

Disappointment jack-knifed through her. 'Not now?'

He bent until their foreheads touched. His smiling eyes still held the same frustration she felt. 'We can if you really want to—but it will wreck my surprise for you.'

Despite her body's screaming need, her eyes lit up. 'Another one? What is it?'

He chuckled. 'If I told you it wouldn't be a surprise—and I think I've been answered. Let's go down for dinner.'

Her gaze searched his face. 'Mark...I didn't mean to...'

A finger touched her mouth, silencing her. 'I'm the one who stopped, not you.'

'Did—did I...?'

A rueful grin touched his mouth. 'Yes, sweetheart, you did. More than any woman I've known since Chloe.'

She held in a gasp. It was the first time he'd said Chloe's name to her—and another thrill, almost painful in its intensity, shivered through her body. 'Are you all right?'

'I'll survive.' He kissed her nose. 'Whether we make love tonight or not.' He must have seen the doubt in her eyes, for his face turned serious. 'Men only say they can't control their reactions so they rouse a woman's guilt, Sylvie, make her give in—or they blame her for what they've done. A real man—one who truly cares about the woman he's with—can wait for her to be ready. Even if it's painful at times.' His grin became more rueful, laughing. 'Like now, in my current predicament. But I can wait for you,' he finished, soft with meaning.

A lump filled her throat and wouldn't be swallowed down. 'I care about you, too,' she whispered. *I love you. I adore you.*

Then tell him the truth, her conscience murmured persistently.

Soon... But I can't tell him now and ruin our night. Please let me hold it back another day. Just one more memory with him...

Mark held out his arm to her. 'Shall we go?'

Trying to tamp down the love shimmering in her eyes and heart, she put her arm through his and they headed out into the soft, heady tropical night.

After an indescribably delicious meal, and a

'torte from heaven' which they'd shared—one plate, two forks—Mark stood and held out his hand to her. 'No lesson tonight,' was all he said. 'No waltzing. Just you and me.'

She rose and moved into his arms, and they swayed together on the shining parquet dance floor with barely a whisper of air between them.

She'd spent so many years working out the one perfect moment for them, and the rare times she'd found herself this close to Mark in her dreams it *had* been perfect. And here they were: Mark in the tuxedo of a prince, she in a golden-ivory dress fit for a princess, and they were on the dance floor.

It wasn't quite perfect. This wasn't a ball, they weren't waltzing, and the crown of her girlish fantasies was missing. But she was locked in his arms, and he was looking at her as if she was beautiful and special—all the things she knew she'd never be…but he believed it.

This was a moment in her life that reached higher than even the most perfect dream.

'This has been the happiest day of my life,' she whispered in his ear. 'It only needs one final thing to be perfect.' *Seeing the sun rise in your arms, knowing we're lovers.*

She was ready. Fear, her constant companion,

still stalked her steps—but she knew that in Mark's arms desire and love would conquer the ancient enemy.

'There's still one surprise to go, remember?' he murmured, with a definite teasing twinkle in his eyes. 'You wanted something last week, but I took it away from you.'

She blinked. Right now she couldn't think of a single thing…

At that moment Mark nodded—and the emcee said quietly, 'At the special request of one of our clients, we have a real treat for you tonight, ladies and gentlemen—especially the gentlemen. Please welcome, from Castile via Sydney, the Colchero Dancers!'

Amid muted but polite applause from the startled guests, the soft clicking whirr of castanets and the muted strains of a flamenco guitar filled the air, and the dancers came on stage. With a confident smile a Spanish woman stepped forward. 'Good evening, ladies and gentlemen. I am Isabella,' she crooned into the microphone. 'Tonight the Colchero Dancers will not Flamenco, Salsa or Sarabande. Tonight we'll teach the ladies here the true roots of the Merengue—the dance of passion and excitement.

The Jaleo is a traditional Romany-Spanish dance of desire unfulfilled, danced by a woman to entice her man. Tonight we'll teach you women how to make your man your slave!' Isabella beckoned. 'I call all the ladies to the stage!'

Sylvie gasped, and Mark stepped away from her with a wink. 'Go for it, sweetheart.'

'I c-can't!' she stammered, her eyes clinging to him for reassurance. 'I'll ruin this beautiful dress, and the shoes…'

'As the rock you gave me says, "Believe". And I do, Sylvie—at last, after all these years, I believe. I believe in *you*.' His eyes shone with faith. 'The dress and the shoes are replaceable— the girls will look after you.'

Her mouth fell open and she stared at him in wonder. He'd done all this for her?

'You're making me cry,' she whispered in a choked voice.

'Not now, Ginger,' he said softly. 'Go and dance for me.'

In a daze, she headed towards the stage and walked up the stairs.

'So we have you here at last,' a laughing female voice, heavily accented, whispered to her. 'We saw it last week—our old friend Marco has finally found the one to melt the ice in his soul—but your passion still only simmers; we can show you how to bring it to fruition. He flew us here first-class last night, with a week's accommodation, so he could make his woman happy. So, come—you will dance for your man!'

Within moments she was transformed. They wound a red scarf in her hair, put hoops in her ears and red lipstick on her mouth; they sprayed her with rose scent. They hitched up the skirt of her dress, holding it up with another sash. 'Instruments of torture,' the woman who'd introduced herself as Isabella said in disgust as she pulled off Sylvie's beautiful shoes. 'You will dance barefoot.'

'But…but…' Sylvie stammered. *My shoes, my shoes*!

Isabella covered Sylvie's lips with a finger. 'I have watched you—both last week and here. You glow when you are in his arms. Your eyes ache. You want this man, yes? You want to be his lover?'

Sylvie gulped, bit her lip. 'Yes,' she finally whispered.

'Then learn from the best. Seduction begins with the foot. Come, you are ready to learn.' Isabella drew her to the front of the stage and the other women surrounded her. She clicked her fingers and the sensuous melody of Spanish guitar filled the air again.

'Follow us,' Isabella whispered to Sylvie as she took her place, shoving two castanets in her hands.

The music changed, became dark and throbbing with abandoned sensuality. The women lifted their arms to the sky, throwing their heads back, making a low, throaty growl as one.

If she ran off now she'd look like a frightened rabbit—but dancing beside these women, so effortlessly fluid and lovely, she'd probably look like a send-up. She shot a helpless glance at Mark, weighing her choices in a moment.

Then she saw the heated flash in his eyes as he looked at her, and it made the decision for her. She followed Isabella's movements.

Then she was too entranced to care if she looked foolish. Enthralled by the beat, by the beauty of the movements, she let herself be swept away into doing what her heart screamed at her to do. She swivelled her hips, pointed her bare feet and clicked the castanets, lifted her head and threw sleepy-eyed looks at Mark, hoping she looked somewhere near as enticing as the other women.

'Beautiful, beautiful,' Isabella murmured with a smile as the dance progressed. 'You are a natural dancer, and your movements are very sensual.'

After that she no longer worried about being silly or clumsy. She felt fluid, sensuous and *confident*. A woman at last....

The rose scent filled her head; the promise of the beat made her feel bold—a woman who knew what to do for the first time. It was as if she'd been stumbling around half-asleep all her life, and with the music and dance came an awakening of her spirit in time with the pulses and the clicks, and the clapping and *olés* of the men, who'd been transformed from rich, polite gentlemen to raw, primitive males from the moment the women began moving.

Tonight Sylvie was truly *alive*. Tonight she was bold and sensual, in thrall to the music, in ecstasy for the only man she'd ever dreamed of. And he was here, *here* with her at last, watching her dance with deep, abiding desire....

'Go dance around your table,' Isabella said softly as she danced past her. 'Your man looks only at you. He is ready for his woman.'

Without even pausing, she turned and danced

her way down the stairs, towards the table. She paused as Mark rose to his feet, his gaze fixed on her, then she moved one final step, lifting her arms again to click the castanets. She reached him, standing at their shadowed corner table, stood before him, and clicked one final time. And she looked at him, hurting with desire and need.

His eyes were dark with restrained passion. 'Let's go,' he muttered, his voice taut. 'Leave the shoes. Someone will bring them back to your room.' Holding her hand, he led her to the secluded cove in front of their cottages, took off his shoes and said, 'Let's walk.' His voice sounded strangled.

Having expected to be in her cottage with a closed door by now, she had to swallow her sick disappointment. But he'd made her day perfect. All she could do was nod. If he wanted to walk, she would.

The islands of the Great Barrier Reef rarely had waves, protected by the massive coral shelf that cut the waters from the Tasman Sea, but tiny eddies came in, with soft *whoosh* sounds, and moonlight danced on the little white bubbles of their peaks. Palm trees hung over the sand. Little hermit crabs flipped over and dug frantic holes to hide as they approached.

It was a magical scene—but right now there was only one kind of magic she wanted…

After a few minutes, desperation overcame scruples, fear and even pride, and she swung around in front of him. 'Did I do it wrong, Mark?'

'Hell, no.' As if her words had released some coiled tension in him, he dragged her against him and buried his face in her hair.

'Then what is it?'

'You know what I said about men and control? I think I lied. Because I'm way past that point now,' he rasped.

Her fears evaporated in pure tenderness. 'And that's a problem because…?'

He pulled back and stared into her eyes, his wild. 'Because you deserve your first real time to be slow, beautiful and perfect. And right now I want to bury myself in you over and over until I can't breathe.'

Sylvie drank him in, masculine and strong and beautiful, and out of control because of her…and she wrapped her arms around his waist. 'You just made this day perfect,' she whispered. 'I couldn't believe I'd drive any man wild with desire, let alone you. But—' she pulled back an inch, and lifted her gaze to him '—tonight, I believe.'

'Ah, sweetheart, you'd better believe.' He leaned in to her until their bodies touched. 'Do you want me?' he murmured in her ear, rough and hot.

Her palms and fingers and every nerve in her body were in pain, straining towards him. 'Yes, *yes*,' she whispered, aching to touch naked skin, to kiss his body.

'Then seduce me, Sylvie.' His voice was deep and taut, dark and lush, hot as a summer night before a storm. The heated current of want moved from his body to hers, and back again.

'I don't know how—that dance was all I had,' she blurted, feeling like the world's biggest fool. Stupid, infatuated girl–fighting for love without any weapons.

He laughed then, low and sensual, and he moved against her, showing her how aroused he was. 'If you don't know how, sweetheart, I can't wait to see you armed with full knowledge. That dance hit me like a bomb. I've wanted you since you first smiled at me—in your pyjamas, your shorts, when you waltz, when you were swimming, in your dress tonight. I love the way you never back down with me—and that dance... In a few weeks you've woken me up from this living death. You turn me inside out and upside down, and you make me want to live. I've been fighting it, but what you do to me all the time… Ah, you've turned me incoherent.' His lips brushed her ear as he spoke, and she shuddered with so many years of waiting for this moment. 'Just say, *I want you, Mark. Make love to me. That's all it takes.*'

'Oh…' It was a soft cry of passion, an admission of everything she'd felt for him for more than two-thirds of her life—for a lonely child's romantic prince, a woman's first and only love. And at last—oh, thank heaven—*at last* they were here, at this moment. 'I want you, I want you.' She touched her fingers to his neck, drew him to her as she went up on tiptoe, whispered, 'Make love to me, Mark,' and kissed him.

As he pulled her up against him, up into his arms, and carried her into the cottage, kissing her with a smiling tenderness that left her melted with desire, happiness, need and love, echoes of past warnings came to her: *Stop wishing for the moon, Sylvie. He's way out of your league now…and you'd probably be disappointed anyway. He's just another man.*

But here I am with the moon in my hands, she thought, thrilling to every touch.

And then Mark laid her down on the bed and lay beside her, deepening his kiss to the passion she'd feared and craved for so long. He touched her face, tumbled her hair with his fingers, caressed her throat as he kissed her, wild and hot and deep. Weeks of gentle kisses turned primal, and because it was Mark she was with him all the way. Her body arched up to his; she moaned, her hands pulling at his tie, tugging at his shirt buttons, pulling his shirt off to kiss his shoulders. Every rational thought had long since fled. Everything was *him*—every thought and movement of her body, every wildly pulsing beat of her heart. *Mark, Mark...*

Then urgent hands pulled her dress up over her hips—and without warning she felt another pair of hands, eager and rough, yanking her school uniform over her stunned, trembling body, grabbing at her untouched breasts with greedy hands older than her father's. Her next-door neighbour, a trusted friend who'd saved them from being thrown out of their house, who'd paid the rent when she'd run out of money, had asked her to clean his house while his wife visited her mother. It would be such a nice surprise for her, wouldn't it?

'You knew what you were doing when you took that five hundred from me. You knew what I wanted when I asked you here today!'

Pain like a knife, splitting her in two. She was going to die…

The next thing she knew she was hitting back, flailing with clenched fists. Screaming incoherent cries of denial, writhing against him in the most elemental instinct to self-protect, to survive.

'Sylvie, it's me. It's Mark. It's all right. We won't do anything you don't want to do,' a beloved voice gasped. And as if a red mist had cleared, she came back to here and now.

To her horror she was kneeling over Mark on the luxurious king-sized bed, hitting him in the chest and stomach. He wasn't holding her fists or pinning her down, but letting her punch him.

'Mark!' she cried, and burst into tears against his chest. 'I'm sorry. *I'm sorry.*'

His arms came around her, fiercely tender, utterly protective, and he let her cry it out. 'You have nothing to apologise for, sweetheart. I think you've needed to let that out for a very long time.' His hands brushed the hair from her face; sombre eyes looked into hers. 'You didn't fight him, did you? What was it he held over you?'

She shuddered. *'I'll call the police and tell them you stole the money. Can you tell them where that five hundred magically came from? Your sick father and those little brothers of yours will be out on the street by tomorrow.'*

'Please,' she whispered, shaking against him, burrowing in for warmth in a world gone suddenly dark and cold.

He held her still in that protective tenderness. 'You've never spoken of this to anyone, have you?'

No, her lips mouthed, but she couldn't say it.

'Simon found you—after?' he guessed, his voice bleak.

She nodded, shuddering with the memory of *how* her brother had found her.

'It's time, sweetheart. The weight of your pain is burying you. *He's* burying you. Don't let him keep holding this power over your life. You have to talk to someone. I'm here, Sylvie,' he said quietly, brushing her tears away with his thumbs.

He's burying you.

With those words, something happened to her: she saw that by her silence, by never letting any man close, her attacker kept on winning the same victory. She'd keep on moving from place to place, looking after others but never meeting her own needs because she didn't deserve it.

'I'm here,' Mark said, kissing her forehead with so much tenderness that more tears rushed to her eyes.

Not for much longer. She closed her eyes, letting the tears fall, and said it—in the same blunt, hard way Mr Landsedge had said it to her all those years ago. 'It wasn't rape.' Was that her voice, croaking like a magpie? 'I sold my virginity for five hundred dollars.'

CHAPTER ELEVEN

ONCE you've sold your soul to survive, you can never have it back.

Finally he understood.

Mark looked at the white face, the make-up streaked with her tears, her eyes nearly black with self-loathing, and he saw the unbearable burden carried on those delicate shoulders for far too long. His heart almost burst with tenderness, but his love wouldn't help her now. She needed catharsis.

'Tell me,' he said quietly.

Her lashes dropped down over her eyes; she laced and unlaced her fingers. 'He was our neighbour. Mr Landsedge. He'd always been—kind. Offered to help out when things got hard for us.'

I just bet he did, Mark thought in blood-red fury, thinking thoughts of vengeance that wouldn't help her.

'What happened?' he asked, refusing to let her dwell on the 'kindness' of the dirty jerk. Child abusers were often very kind and helpful—until they reached their target. Then threats and lies became their stock-in-trade to avoid prosecution.

'One month, when Dad had been really sick, we needed money desperately or we'd be tossed out of the house. Welfare would split us up. He—he came to me and offered to pay a full month's rent to help us out of the hole.'

Noting the creep hadn't approached her father, who probably would have guessed what was going on, Mark said again, 'Tell me.'

She gave a shuddering sigh. 'He asked me to clean their house as—as a surprise for his wife when she came home from visiting her mother. Of course I did it. Of course,' she repeated, with a weary sadness more heartbreaking than any bitterness could be. 'And—and then he said he needed the money back. I didn't have it.' Pleading eyes lifted to his, begging in silence for him to understand, holding an underlying hopeless-ness—and he knew what she was thinking. How could he understand what she'd done when she still didn't? 'I—I offered to pay it by the week. I offered to clean the house every week for a year.

But—but…' She shuddered and buried her face in her hands. 'He caught me in the spare bedroom. He tore my school uniform—the only— only one I had,' she mumbled, her voice lifting by octaves to a half-wail as she cried through her fingers. 'He said I'd known what he wanted when I took the money. He said my coming over was agreeing to—to…selling my virginity. He said it was obvious I'd *enjoyed* it.' She shuddered again. 'I thought I was going to tear in two, and—and then he tried to make a date to do it again the next week!'

A red mist covered his eyes, blood-red and pulsing with fury against the unnameable piece of filth who'd hurt his beautiful little Mary so badly she'd stopped being Mary.

I'm going to find the creep and—

'I'm sorry. I'll go now.'

The pathetic little whisper, her scramble to get off his bed, snapped him out of his wrath. How long had he been sitting there thinking about Landsedge while Sylvie waited for his reaction in growing hopelessness?

'Sweetheart?'

The word, soaked in all the love he felt bursting from his heart, stopped her clumsy flight. But she didn't look at him. Her back was stiff and straight, as it had been the day her mother died—when she'd faced a future filled with burdens all on her own.

She expected him to walk away.

'What happened next?'

A long, slow quiver ran through her, but still she stood straight and proud. 'I…I was sick. I couldn't get out of bed for two weeks. I couldn't even help the boys. He—he tried to be helpful again. He came in my room.' She sniffed, and said simply, 'I whacked him in the face with Drew's baseball bat.'

A startled laugh burst from him before he could smother it. 'That's my girl.'

She half twisted towards him, but then turned back again. 'I broke his nose,' she said, flat and hard. 'I told him if he came near me again I'd tell his wife. He said I knew where to come the next time I needed "financial help", and that he knew I'd come.' She stood trembling, and his gut twisted with a cocktail of murderous fury, compassion, love and a fierce pride in her. 'Then, two weeks later, *you* came to our rescue. I took five hundred out as soon as I could. I saw him in his garden and threw it in his face. Then I grabbed his shears and hacked off all his prize roses. The neighbours were watching. He didn't know what to do. I yelled that if he ever came near me again I'd go to the police.'

'What else happened, sweetheart?' he asked quietly, sensing the story wasn't over.

She sighed. 'Simon found me trying to get in the house with rips in my uniform without anyone seeing. After…'

He shot to his feet, crossed to her and pulled her close. 'Sylvie. Oh, sweetheart.'

She didn't move or react to his touch, stood stiff and cold. 'Simon told Mrs Landsedge, who believed it because of the broken nose and the way Simon and I refused to talk to him or look at him. She kicked him out. All the money was hers.'

A very neat revenge—as long as a probably still furious, vengeful but currently powerless Mr Landsedge never discovered she was now dating a very rich man and made his grubby version of the story public. *Mark Hannaford's girlfriend sold me her virginity for five hundred dollars.*

Now he knew why Sylvie refused to go anywhere where they might be noticed by the press. She was protecting him, protecting her family—and herself, of course. But he knew she'd put herself last, as usual. He'd never met anyone as loving and giving as Sylvie, and she set such a low value on herself.

Thinking quickly, he knew what he had to do. Sylvie would never tell this story to an outsider; it was her way. He was pretty well certain even Simon didn't know the whole story, either. He was so protective of his sister—if he knew what she'd done to save them…

It was up to him, then—and he racked his brain for the research he'd done on the subject when a female employee had recovered memories of childhood abuse and been too traumatised to work for months.

'Do you remember what I said about men and control?' He caressed those shining tumbled curls.

She looked up, a small light of laughter in her eyes. 'Duh. You said it three hours ago.'

He chuckled and kissed her forehead, so proud of her ability to laugh—she was a survivor, his Sylvie. 'Men who have no respect for women also lie about their reasons for forcing a woman—or a child—to make it appear to be her fault.' He lifted her chin with a finger, then cupped her face in his hands. 'He set you up, sweetheart. He chose you because you were vulnerable in your love for your family—and he manipulated events to get what he wanted. And when he knew you might go to the police he found a way to make you feel ashamed and scared. He made you feel like a prostitute so you wouldn't tell.'

After a long silence, he added, 'You didn't sell a thing, Sylvie. You were a child. All the responsibility for this *crime* belongs to him. He hurt you, lied to you and manipulated you so you wouldn't do the one thing he feared—go to the police.'

She gave a shuddering sigh, looking at him in pure wonder. 'You don't despise me?'

Gently he kissed her mouth. 'Never, sweetheart. Even if you'd been forced to become what you feared most I couldn't hate you.' He sighed. 'If anything, you should despise *me*. I've treated women badly for too many years. Until you came back to me women were a way to put another Band-Aid on a wound that wouldn't heal, to forget what I'd become. I didn't pay them, but in every other way I treated them with less respect than they deserved.' He looked in her eyes with total seriousness. 'It's not my forgiveness you need, Sylvie. You don't even need to forgive yourself. You need to see that you never did anything wrong.'

'Not—not even when I broke his nose?'

He nuzzled her hair with his mouth. 'Especially not that.'

With a tiny muffled sound she buried her face in his chest. 'I was so scared you'd hate me. I couldn't bear it if you hated me.'

And at last he knew the time had come to speak. 'I have no right to despise you. You're innocent of everything but trusting the wrong person.' He dropped his hands as the shutters fell away from his soul. 'It's me who's never had the right to be with *you*.' He refused to turn away, looking into her eyes with all the self-condemnation he deserved. 'You think I'm an alcoholic, don't you?'

With confusion in her eyes, she nodded.

'I'm not—well, not in the traditional sense.' He took her hand and led her to the two seats near the sliding-glass doors overlooking the ocean. 'After Chloe died,' he said deliberately, 'I went nuts. I skipped school. I got drunk to forget. My parents could barely find me to stop me. I only came home to sleep, or to take more money out of the bank. I wasted years of careful saving for university on drink and a cheap car. I lived in the car, and I kept playing chicken with red lights, screeching around corners. I wanted to die and join her.'

She said nothing, her gaze fixed on his face, waiting for the rest. Her beautiful old-sherry eyes were full of compassion, love and faith.

It was the worst possible moment to realise she was in love with him, that *he* was the prince she'd spoken of...

He went on in a hard voice, refusing to hide a single part of the missing year of his life. 'My family and Chloe's tried so hard to help me. They tried everything—from taking me to a counselor, to locking me in to saying she'd be ashamed of me. I didn't care. She shouldn't have left me, but since she had, all I wanted was to be with her. Eventually they closed my bank account. I got a job delivering pizzas and used the money to drink. The wonder of it is I never used drugs—but maybe I knew Chloe would really despise me for that. And yet something in me kept saying, *If Mary can keep going, why can't you?* Somehow your memory kept me from killing myself. Either with drugs or any other way.'

'I'm glad,' she said softly, her whole face alight

with love, and he ached to touch her, to tell her he loved her, adored her…

So he told her the worst thing—blurting it out to stop himself from ruining her life with his need for her. 'Then I turned the wrong corner at the wrong time—too fast, too drunk. I hit a kid on a bike.'

She gasped. 'Was he all right?'

The distancing had already begun, and he couldn't blame her. 'Robbie spent the next five months in hospital, with multiple fractures in his legs and hip, arm and skull.'

'Robbie?'

'Allsopp,' he added with a nod.

'So…you stayed at the accident scene? You didn't run?'

'Of course not,' he snarled, but he knew she was right to ask. After all he'd done, why wouldn't he have played the coward's part and run?

Deflated, he said quietly, 'It woke me up. I wanted to kill *me*, not someone else. Then in the hospital—I fractured my arm—my family rallied around me, doing what they could for the Allsopps, too. I finally saw what I was doing—not just to me, but to everyone around me.' He sighed. 'I called the Allsopps every day, asking how Robbie was, begging forgiveness. They—were kind.' He dropped his head onto his hand. 'I couldn't believe it, but they forgave me. Robbie forgave me. The only thing they asked was that I get help.'

'And you did.' It wasn't a question. She knew he had.

He nodded. 'I went into rehab even before the case came to court. Because I'd gone in voluntarily and the counsellors said I was truly repentant, and when even the Allsopps came to testify for me, as well as against me, the judge was compassionate. He said my history showed I wasn't a delinquent and I was already in a rehabilitation facility. He recommended I never drink again. When I swore I wouldn't, he only took my driver's licence for two years. I didn't care about that. I'd already used the insurance on the car to pay for a little of Robbie's health needs. My parents sold their house to pay for the rest, and for my rehab.' He said simply, 'I was six months off turning eighteen. Being a minor, the files on me are sealed. It's the only reason the story never made the tabloids.'

'Where's Robbie now?' she asked gently. 'Don't tell me you don't know. I won't believe you. I *know* you've paid your debt there. In fact, I'm willing to bet you did that before you bought your parents their new house, or bought that second-hand car for yourself when you patented Howlcat.'

He looked up with a half-grin; how well she knew him. 'He's a physiotherapist. He says the accident showed him what he wanted to do—to help others through what happened to him. Maggie and Sean, his parents, say the accident gave him empathy for others' suffering.'

'As it did you,' she murmured, laying her hand on his.

He withdrew his hand. 'Don't be kind to me, Sylvie. I don't deserve your praise. I only did what I had to do.'

'At *seventeen*,' she said with soft emphasis. 'If I was a child, so were you. You'd lost the love of your life too young. You became a widower *at seventeen*. After five years of being strong, giving and responsible, doing everything right, suddenly you had nothing to do, nowhere to be. School was empty, because she wasn't there. Inventing just reminded you of her. You were like a spring held down too long, released to nothing—you just bounced all over the place. You became a teenage boy for the first time, doing stupid things without thinking of the consequences to others—and it's a time you obviously regret and will never repeat.' She came around the table between them and squatted before him. 'You've become a strong, fine, giving man who doesn't blow his trumpet. You have the forgiveness of those who matter. It's not *my* forgiveness you need,' she said, repeating what he'd told her only ten minutes ago. 'You need to forgive yourself.'

Unable to stand any more of her tender reassurance—it was too *tempting* to believe her—he jerked to his feet. 'I *can't*.' He pulled open the door. Without looking at her, he snarled, 'I know what you want to say. Don't do it. Don't love me, Sylvie. It's not worth it. *I'm* not worth it.'

As he headed for his cottage to change, desperately needing time out, he heard her murmur, soft and sad, 'It's years too late to tell me that.'

CHAPTER TWELVE

A week later

IN a beautiful bridesmaid's dress of soft apricot-pink that made her look more than ever like the hated china doll, smiling for friends and family, Sylvie walked down the aisle of the old church in the neighbourhood where they'd all grown up.

It was Scott and Sarah's big day, and she wasn't about to ruin it for them.

Even if she couldn't stop thinking of Mark the whole time, wondering where he'd been since they came home from Turtle Island. He hadn't come home, hadn't gone to work. He'd dropped her off in the limo and said he needed to get away. 'It's not you, it's me,' he'd said, in the time-worn phrase that always made women feel unloved and inadequate. He'd never left Chloe for a minute— no matter how much he'd needed to get away…

On the way home in the jet, she'd asked him to be her partner for the wedding. He'd said, 'I'd be honoured,' sounding anything but happy about it.

Then she'd made the monumental mistake of saying she loved him. His silence had filled her with terror. She'd added hastily that she expected nothing from him—yet still he'd disappeared.

He hadn't shown up for the wedding. He wasn't coming.

She heard the words of love, commitment and shared faith between her two dearest friends with a lump in her throat. She hugged and kissed them and said she was so happy—and she *was*—but she felt like a liar. She took Angelo's arm on the way down the aisle, posed for the obligatory photos and rode to the reception hall with him, applauded the bride and groom's entrance. She ate almost nothing of her dinner, pretending it was because she was smiling and laughing too much.

The tears of a clown beneath.

Then came the time for the bridal waltz. Without thinking about it, Sylvie left her seat and walked down the stairs from the high table, waiting for Angelo on the dance floor.

She waited—and waited. She turned to the table—he'd disappeared. She threw a frantic look at Sandi, his fiancée, who lifted her hands in the air in awkward apology.

Angelo had done a runner.

She stood in the middle of the dance floor as Scott and Sarah twirled gracefully around her, her cheeks scorched with humiliation, knowing a dozen video cameras were rolling and this would be a 'funniest home video' moment worth putting on the TV.

She looked around for Simon, Drew and Joel, who were always ready to rescue her…but her brothers just sat there grinning. Why weren't they coming to help her? Surely they could see she was writhing in her public embarrassment?

Then a deep voice said from behind her, 'I believe this is our dance, Miss Browning.'

She swivelled around in astonished joy. *'Mark,'* she whispered, her heart pounding as he took her in his arms in the traditional dance hold. He'd come for her. He'd rescued her again…

She took in the full tuxedo he wore, as if he was one of the bridal party. Careful not to say anything to drive him away again, she could only whisper, 'Thank you—thank you.'

He smiled down at her. 'After what you told me I thought Angelo might bolt, so I came prepared.'

He stepped forward and she moved back in the waltz, and he twirled her, making her feel graceful and pretty. 'I tried to make it on time, but there was traffic on the bridge after an accident.'

'I thought you weren't coming.'

His mouth quirked up. 'You should know me better than that. I've always been there for you. Okay, so sometimes I've been a bit late, but I'm always there.' He took in her outfit. 'You look beautiful.'

She sighed. 'I look like a china doll again.'

'So did Chloe, if you remember,' he said, smiling at her. 'I've always been a sucker for china dolls.'

They danced in silence for a few minutes. Mark seemed content to be quiet. Sylvie had no idea what to say to his comparison of her to Chloe. He'd brought up her name with a smile on his face...

As the floor began to fill up with other wedding guests, he said, 'I guess you're wondering where I've been this week. I know Mum and the girls didn't tell you.'

Hearing the note in his voice—of a *peace* she hadn't heard in it either as a child or a man—she looked up. 'I'm sorry. I shouldn't have called your mother, but I was worried.'

'You can call my family any time, sweetheart.' He tipped her face up and brushed his mouth over hers. 'They all adore you, and they know you only want the best for me.'

At that, she lost control over her aching heart and runaway mouth. Shaking her head, she looked down and away. 'No. I want a lot of things—not only what's best for you.' She gulped and went on, feeling totally hopeless. 'I'm sorry, Mark. You're so good to me, so *kind,* and I know that I'm not her and I'll never be her, but I can't help it.'

'Can't help what?' he whispered in her ear.

She couldn't look up as she murmured in an anguished voice, 'Loving you so much.'

He dropped his hand from hers and her heart lurched—but then he wrapped his arm around her waist, drawing her tight against him. 'You don't hate me for what I did?'

She sighed. 'Nothing will change the way I feel, Mark. I've loved you since the day I first saw you. I know you don't want it—'

'Who says I don't want it?' he asked softly.

'Don't be kind to me,' she said with a gritted-teeth smile, remembering she was maid of honour, and they were surrounded by a crowd of happy dancers and photographers. 'Don't call me sweetheart. It makes me hope for things I can't have with you.'

'Why can't you have them? Why can't you have me?'

'Stop it!' she cried, forgetting everything but her pain. She tried to move out of his arms, but he held her in a deadlock. 'Please stop. I know you're *fond* of me—of little Shirley Temple. I know you want my friendship, want to take care of me just like you always have. You know I love you and you want me to be happy—'

'Correction,' he interrupted in a gentle voice. 'I want *us* to be happy. Yes, I want to take care of you. Yes, I know you love me. And, yes, I'm *fond* of Shirley Temple. I always have been. But that's in the past.'

'So's Chloe, and you still love *her*!'

'True,' he admitted without hesitation. 'I'm a faithful kind of man. Once I love, I can't change.'

'Then think how *painful* it would be for you if she was here now but she didn't love you the way you want her to!'

For the third time in as many minutes, he bent to her ear. 'Who says I don't love you the way you want me to?'

She stilled so suddenly he tripped over her motionless feet, almost taking her down onto the floor. He righted himself with her quick hands.

'That's my girl—always helping me up when I'm down,' he murmured, and took her back in his arms, dancing with a slow sensuality that made her insides feel like melted chocolate, liquid, hot and sweet, and so filled with love she could barely breathe.

'What did you say?' she asked in an anguished whisper.

He didn't pretend to misunderstand or tease her. 'I said I love you, Mary Brown/Sylvie Browning—exactly the way you want me to. There's just one thing wrong with your name-change,' he said softly. 'It should be Hannaford. But it will be when you marry me.'

The words she'd waited a lifetime to hear. Again, it wasn't the stuff of her dreams—not the long, romantic declaration she'd wanted. But when she looked in his eyes she saw not a fairy-tale prince but a man in love....

And she began hyperventilating, wheezing with each laboured breath.

Concerned friends and family began crowding around. Simon, Drew and Joel, all dancing nearby, shouldered their way through to where they stood.

'What did you do to her?' Simon demanded of Mark, with the fierceness he always used to protect her from the world, covering his anxieties with anger the way she did with a smile. 'You said to trust you with her, and now she's—'

'No need to worry, Simon.' Mark broke into Simon's tirade with a calm smile. 'It's marriage-proposal shock, that's all. She'll be fine in a minute.'

Her brothers were silent for about three seconds, then all three burst out laughing. 'She did it,' Drew said in a dazed voice. 'I can't believe she did it!'

'You should have known she would,' Mark said, doing the palm thing on her back she'd done with his hiccups. 'You can welcome me to the family when she's coherent enough to say yes. Excuse us now. We need some privacy.'

Amid her brothers' amazed chuckles and the understanding smiles of her friends, he lifted her up in his arms and carried her out into the warm, late-summer night to the garden surrounding the reception building. He sat on a bench amid a section of roses and held her with that cherishing tenderness she could never resist. 'So, are you going to keep me hanging?

Or are you going to say *Yes, Mark, I'll marry you and I love you*?'

She felt the familiar stinging of her eyes. How he could bring her to tears so fast she'd never know. 'You love Chloe. You said it.'

'Yes, I do. I always will. Part of me will always miss her—she was my best friend, my inventing partner, the love of the boy I was. But she's been gone half a lifetime, and I'm not *in* love with her any more. I'm in love with you.' He trailed his lips over her cheek, her hair, her mouth. 'I think that was the reason I was so cold and uncaring all those years. I didn't realise that as I was losing Chloe you'd already come into my life and filled my heart. I spent all those years waiting for you to come back to me.'

She blinked, but found no words to say.

He smiled down at her and caressed her cheek. 'I think that's why Chloe foisted that impossible promise on us both, you know.'

Her brow crinkled. 'Why?'

'To bring us back together. She knew what we didn't.' He bent and kissed her again. 'All the things I loved about her she saw in you: the adorable stubbornness, the refusal to give up on me, always seeing the best in me, loving me no matter what. I think she knew what would happen to me without her—so she sent you to me. I thought I'd gone so cold because I'd lost Chloe, but it started months, even years before she died. It began when she was first diagnosed with cancer. Because I was going to lose her, to be alone, I became cold with every person outside the family circle. Holding off from the world was my protection against the pain. But with you I couldn't be hard or cold. You were too special to me.' His fingers trailed along her jaw, and she shivered with the power of it, the beauty. 'When she died and you left my life the sunshine disappeared. Even after I came out of rehab life felt bleak. The coldness never left me—no matter what I invented, what I could do for others, what woman I was with, or what level of success I reached.' He added softly, 'Then you came back to me. I felt the change at my first sight of you. I'm not the Heart of Ice now because of you. You melted me, Sylvie. You *melted* me.'

And *that* was why she could never wear make-up around him. 'You melt me, too—obviously,' she wailed, and hiccupped, tears streaking paths through her professionally done face. 'What about the press—the story about me?'

'I found Landsedge this week,' he said grimly. 'He's not worth it, sweetheart. Since his wife kicked him out he's become a pathetic old man in a nursing home. He's got early-onset dementia. If he sells his story—which I doubt, because when I saw him he didn't know what day it was or remember your name—we'll survive it together.'

She nodded, touched that he'd gone to such lengths to reassure her. 'I—might have other problems,' she whispered. 'When we—'

'I know, sweetheart.' He kissed her with sweet lingering. 'If you want to know where I went this week, I went to see Robbie, his parents—and I saw my old counsellor. She runs her own private clinic. She'd like to meet you. She's been where you are,' he added, when she made an instinctive movement of withdrawal. 'Amanda knows the shame and the fear. She doesn't think you need her help, sweetheart—and she says you did for me what she couldn't, because our trust in each other is absolute.' After a moment in which she had no idea what to say, he added, 'You were right, Sylvie. I told Amanda what you said about learning to forgive myself.' He brushed his mouth over hers once, twice. 'She said if I didn't marry you I'd be making the biggest mistake of my life, whether I believe I'm worthy of you or not. She said you're obviously a very intelligent and strong woman, and perfect for me.'

The indecision and fear receded. If Mark could face his worst nightmares, if he could see a counsellor for her sake and be willing to go with her, couldn't she be strong enough to go with him?

'Did you make an appointment?'

'Monday at 4:00 p.m.' He hugged her. 'Thank you, sweetheart. I knew you could do it.'

'Kiss me,' she said, lifting her face to his.

'You still haven't answered me. *Yes, I'll marry you, Mark. I love you, Mark,*' he parroted in soft insistence. 'No kisses until we're engaged.'

'You've been kissing me this whole time,' she pointed out, feeling her entire body shining with happiness.

He rolled his eyes, laughing. 'Okay, then, no *more* kisses until we're engaged. Now, say it, woman— or I swear I'll make you so crazy for me—'

She already was. Insanely in love… She whispered, 'Yes, Mark, I'll marry you. I love you so much. You were my first crush and you became my only love—the only man I've ever wanted or will ever want.' She smiled up at him. 'I've gone a whole week without touching you. Now, *please* kiss me—and you couldn't make me any crazier for you. You do that to me just by being alive,' she said softly.

'One more thing first.' He smiled, and pulled out a tiny box from his jacket pocket. He flipped it open and lifted the antique rose-gold ring out. It was studded with one sweet ruby, flanked by two little diamonds each side. 'It was my Grandma Hannaford's,' he said softly. 'Grandad said when he gave it to her that it was his reminder that he had a woman worth more than rubies. When she died twelve years ago he gave up. He gave the ring to me before he died; Grandma wanted me to have it. He said when I found a woman as price-less as Grandma, one worth spending every day of my life with, I'd know what to do.'

'Oh, *look* what you've made me do,' she wailed, as more tears ruined her make-up. She held out her left hand while swiping at her face with the right.

'I love you,' he whispered, and slid the ring on her finger. Then, at last, he kissed her—deep and slow and filled with love.

Much later, they heard loud voices complain-ing that first the best man disappeared for the bridal waltz, and now the maid of honour hadn't shown up for photos. They smiled at each other, and Mark pulled out a handkerchief, wiping off the mess of tear-streaked make-up.

'You're far prettier without it, anyway.' Then he lifted her to her feet. 'Go on in there, wife. You're needed.'

Wife… She promptly melted again. 'This is our engagement night. Come with me. We need a photo or three for our grandchildren to smile at one day.'

As they walked hand in hand up the stairs he asked, 'So, when do we want the wedding, and where?'

She squeezed his hand. 'You know where. There's only one place for us, Mark, if Chloe's memory is to be part of our day. And she deserves that tribute.'

He turned to her, eyes dark with emotion. 'Perfect.' His voice cracked on the word, and he led her inside to raucous congratulations as he became part of her family.

The garden, St Agatha's Hospice,
two months later

The stereo began playing the beautiful romantic thirties music they both loved, and Mark, flanked by Pete, Glenn, Drew and Joel, turned to see his bride.

Sylvie's friend Sarah led the procession, followed by Bren, Becky and Katie, down past the few standing guests that would fit in this little garden where they'd first met.

Then Sylvie came out on Simon's arm, wearing her mother's wedding dress, Mark's mother's silk wedding slippers, Mark's grandmother's ring and Bren's veil.

The dress was a plain slip of silk with an old-fashioned ivory lace overdress, falling straight to her feet in a hippie style; her hair was loose, shining through the gossamer veil. And her face was so radiant with joy and love it shone through the dainty lace covering her. Her gaze never wavered from him.

You may not feel worthy of her love, but she's given her heart and trust to you—only you, his heart whispered. *So make yourself worthy of her. Don't let her down.*

Mark almost couldn't breathe because he felt so choked up with love. She was walking down the aisle to him, the embodiment of everything he'd never believed he could have—and she loved him, with all his faults and private and public baggage. She trusted him with her future.

She reached his side; Simon lifted her veil and

kissed her. Drew and Joel came around Mark and followed suit, not in rehearsed symphony, but as brothers who adored her, sharing in the joy of her day. She hugged them and said, 'I love you,' and they said it back.

Sylvie turned to Mark and took his hands in hers. 'Smile,' she said softly.

The light and warmth of her presence and touch filled him again; the shining happiness that was Sylvie streaked through his body.

'That's better.' She winked at him and they turned to the celebrant, his cousin Ryan, who married them with the same deep, abiding delight of the entire Hannaford clan.

Even Chloe's parents were here, so happy for Mark…

As Sylvie made her vows Mark drank in every word—and yet he heard a soft, feminine echo from the past. *'Promise me you'll be happy, Mark. Find a girl to love.'*

'They say you can't find lasting love as a child, that you'll forget,' Sylvie said, her hands in his. 'But "they" aren't always right. I've loved you since I was eight years old, and it's only deepened through the years. You were my prince, my hero, my reason to keep living—and now you're my love, my dearest friend, the other half of me. I make you my vow that it will never change, in good times or in bad, in sickness or in health, rich or poor, because it never has.' She smiled up at him, misty with love. 'It's built to last a lifetime.'

He choked up again, marvelling at the devoted love he'd found a second time in his life—and in silence he thanked its source. *You told me to find love again, but you'd already found her for me, hadn't you, Chloe? You always knew me better than I knew myself*, he thought with a smile as Sylvie slid the wedding ring on his finger.

Ryan pronounced them husband and wife, his smile going a fair way to splitting his face. 'Go ahead and kiss her,' he said with a wink.

'Alone at last,' Sylvie said on a contented sigh.

They'd chosen to stay home for their wedding night; Sylvie wanted the familiarity of beloved surroundings for their first time, and Mark felt exactly the same.

Tomorrow they'd fly to the Greek islands and spend their time on a yacht, finding B and Bs to stay in. Tonight was just Mark and Sylvie, in the home they loved.

Mark didn't carry her over the threshold; she

didn't want to start their lives together with superstition.

'I don't need to worry about bad luck, Mark. I've been given enough miracles to know where to put my trust,' she said softly as they walked in the back door hand in hand. 'I think we could both use a cup of tea,' she murmured, when Mark had closed the door.

He could see her hands trembling. 'Just what we both need,' he agreed, aching with love and desire—but the imperative thing was to give Sylvie control, to make her feel safe.

So here they were on their wedding night, husband and wife, drinking tea…

She started talking about the utter joy of their day, uninterrupted by any media hype or circus. 'The photos should be beautiful,' she said, her fingers tapping on the cup.

Mark nodded, letting her babble out her nerves, caressing the hand he held in loving reassurance. They'd contacted and made an exclusive deal with a magazine, donating all funds to his favourite charity, Medicin Sans Frontiers, with the proviso that there would be no announcement made until they went to press, when they would be on their way to Greece. Their photographer was sending the shots tonight, with comments given by the guests and family.

Waiting was becoming an agony now. He'd been patient through the past two months as she'd explored her newfound sensuality and her power over him, knowing he'd always stop when she said, or when she trembled too hard. But she was his wife, he adored her, and—

'So—are we going to bed now?'

The question was a compound of timidity and eagerness. He drank in those beautiful eyes, huge with uncertainty. 'Only if you want to, sweetheart.'

'I do,' she burst out. 'I've wanted to for weeks, but…' She chewed on her thumbnail.

Mark leaned into her, touching his forehead to hers. 'I can wait if you're still not ready, Sylvie. We have a lifetime.' His voice was hard with the strain of saying it.

'What's *wrong* with me?' she cried wretchedly. 'Why am I so scared? I love you so much, Mark. When you touch me I feel so beautiful. I want to be with you.'

He groaned at the words. 'I love you, too. Enough to wait.' His body screamed protest at the words, but he said them for her sake.

She talked over him, as if she hadn't heard. 'But I'm scared of what I'll feel. I couldn't *stand* it if I freaked out and hit you again!'

In all the weeks he'd waited for her she'd never said that—and he almost laughed in the exquisite relief. So ridiculous, so beautiful and so Sylvie— she'd been raped and she still worried about hurting him, putting his welfare above her own, as ever… That was his girl. 'Is that what's been bothering you? Why you've always stopped at that point?'

Her face pale, she nodded, chewing fiercely on the poor abused thumb.

Gently he took her hand from her mouth. 'I can show you ways around that.'

Her mouth fell open. 'Really?'

'Really,' he repeated, thinking tenderly of this girl raised by a man, who'd run a house but had no time to play; whose only personal experience was violent. She was a virgin in all the ways that counted. 'I can show you how to make love to me, Sylvie. You'll be in control all the way.'

He waited for her reaction.

Not for long… Within moments her eyes took fire, she lifted their linked hands and kissed his palm, slow and lingering. 'I want you, Mark. I want to make love.'

Remembering the words from their fateful night at Turtle Island, and the mistakes he'd made in his frantic need for her, he said softly, 'Then take me to bed.'

With a wide smile of delight, she stood and led him up the stairs. 'We can wash up later—after you teach me this new dance,' she said softly, and he chuckled. Tonight they'd dance with the oldest and most beautiful moves known to a man and woman in love.

When they reached the bedroom, he said, 'It starts with a kiss. Kiss me, sweetheart.'

With a half-smile and a full blush, she drew him down for a long, slow kiss. He allowed her to set the pace.

'What now?' she asked breathlessly, when they were both shaking with need.

'You undress me.' If he was the one vulnerable first, naked on the bed, maybe it would give her strength and courage, would arouse and reassure her.

With wide eyes and uncertain hands she worked at his shirt buttons—he'd already discarded the jacket and tie. But before the shirt was off, she whispered, *'Oh...'* in a tone of sensuous wonder and discovery. She peeled the shirt off, her hands caressing his skin, her lips trailing his chest and stomach, growing hotter, fevered. 'Oh, Mark, darling…'

He held on to his ragged threads of self-control. She'd come this far before, become totally aroused and then panicked. 'If you're ready, sweetheart, you can take off my pants.'

Too soon. Stupid, *stupid*! She closed her eyes, looking like a prisoner before a firing squad as she pulled off his belt and undid the button on his pants.

'You might need to take off my shoes first, or I'll fall over when the pants drop,' he whispered, angling for a laugh—and the lovely silver and gold gurgle of her mirth came. Her eyes alight, she bent to his feet and pulled off his shoes and socks. He looked down at her curly head in anguish. He didn't know how much longer he could hold on.

But then she stood and looked in his eyes, and hers were filled with love and trust. 'Now the pants?' Her voice came out as a squeak, but she said it.

'If you're ready,' he said quietly. 'And put me on the bed.'

As he'd hoped, the sight of him on the bed, in a position of vulnerability and trust, aroused

Sylvie so much she fell on him. 'Darling, *darling*,' she murmured, kissing and caressing his body with fevered lips and hands. 'I love you. I want you.'

'I love you, too. Always.' He closed his eyes as her touch drove him to the point of madness. 'If you're ready, take your dress off.' The final power and determination: if she took her dress off, which she'd never allowed him to do without giving in to terror—

'Mark?' she said softly.

He opened his eyes to see Sylvie in her underwear—silky, lacy pieces over tiny curves, exquisite. 'Ah, sweetheart, sweetheart—you're so beautiful,' he croaked. *Reassure her all the way that she's beautiful, loved and in control*, he chanted in his mind. 'My bride, my wife,' he went on, aware he was babbling, sick with nerves that she'd back out.

But he'd stumbled into saying the perfect thing. 'Yes.' She sounded fiercely proud. 'I'm Sylvie Hannaford…and you're my husband, my man.'

'For a lifetime,' he agreed, his voice aching with the desire that was half killing him.

With a sweet, mysterious woman smile, she reached behind her to unhook her bra…

Instinct and love took over; he showed her what to do, and she was too aroused, too soaked in newfound bliss and pleasure, to think of the past. And for the first time in half a lifetime Mark treasured the experience of what it was to truly make love with the woman he'd committed his life to: a woman who adored him, who'd never want to touch any other man.

He was a man doubly blessed in the women he'd loved.

As she lay on him after, he played with her hair while she kissed his damp chest, murmuring words of love and faith, and *for ever*. Of loving, making babies and being a family… They had a lifetime together.

Then she moved against him in unmistakable meaning. 'Can we do that again?'

It wasn't really a question, and as they touched and loved each other's bodies Mark knew that, though they had a way to go, everything would be all right for them from now on.

EPILOGUE

Five years later

MARK let himself in the door of his parents' house to hear the laughter and teasing of a family get-together. 'Hey, I'm back,' he called down the hall.

'Mark!' The voice was Sylvie's, filled with joy. He heard a chair scrape back and awkward steps running to him.

'Don't run, sweetheart,' he said as she burst into the hall, her face alight with love and welcome. 'You know you're not supposed to.' He moved to her with quick strides.

A heavily pregnant Sylvie snuggled into his arms with a deep sigh of contentment. 'Oh, I've missed you. Don't go anywhere without me again.'

'I've only been gone three days.' But he'd missed her, too—so much he'd caught a flight home from Singapore two hours earlier, on a different carrier. At thirty-four weeks pregnant, Sylvie couldn't fly with him, and the trip had been unavoidable, but as far as he was concerned it was the last trip he'd take without his family. A day without Sylvie's smile and touch was a day too long. Even after five years he didn't take her love for granted. Every day was still a miracle to him, her love a gift he didn't deserve but thanked God for.

Her brow lifted. 'You won't think it's *only* three days when it comes to bedtime. Katie slept in Chloe's room while she stayed, and now Madam Princess doesn't see why she can't sleep with *us* every night.'

Mark groaned. 'Oh, great. More bedtime re-education. Thanks, Katie.'

'And that's Daddy's department,' she said, with clear smugness in her tone. 'You're the only one who can get through to her.'

'Stubborn little puss. Her mother's daughter,' he teased with a grin.

'Kiss me,' she whispered fiercely, wrapping her arms around his neck and drawing him down to her. After a long kiss filled with heat, she whispered, 'When can we go home?'

'Can I at least say hi to the family and see my

daughter before you make use of my body?' he mock-complained, loving that even after five years, and only six weeks away from her giving birth, he could arouse her with a touch. Sometimes the past came back to haunt her, but rarely when they made love; it was more on sad anniversaries.

She grumbled, 'Oh, I suppose so.' Her eyes twinkled. 'One more kiss.'

'When are you two gonna get *over* it?' Pete demanded from the door to the dining room. 'Everyone's waiting for dinner.'

Sylvie turned her head and grinned at Pete. 'Never,' she vowed fervently. 'You wouldn't, either, if you had a husband like mine.'

'*Eeew*. I've shared a room with him, remember? I'm definitely over it.'

They chuckled.

'Daddy-Daddy-Daddy-Daddy!'

Mark's grin widened at the frantic call; two-and-a-half-year-old Chloe always said *Daddy* in a blur of 'd's. 'I'm here, princess,' he called to her.

'Here comes the express,' Pete groaned with a grin, and stepped out of the way.

'Daddy-Daddy-Daddy-Daddy-Daddy!'   A

chubby-limbed blonde with a Pebbles hairdo came flying at him, much as Sylvie had done, and crashed into his legs. 'Daddy, I hab *missed* you,' she cried, trying to jump up into his arms.

He chuckled again, and picked her up. She wrapped her little arms tight around his neck, slobbering kisses on his cheek. With her blonde hair and golden-brown eyes Chloe was the image of him, but her personality was all Sylvie. And because he worked from home two days a week, caring for Chloe while Sylvie worked at the hospice, he was close to his daughter. 'I missed you, too, princess.'

'Chloe sleep with Daddy tonight?' she asked hopefully.

Pete sniggered as Mark made a face of helplessness at him. 'Yeah, good luck with that.' And he disappeared back into the dining room.

Sylvie laughed, but said firmly, 'No, pumpkin. Mummy sleeps with Daddy. You can sleep in the same room with the baby when she comes.'

'Baby come now?' Chloe asked, without missing a beat.

Mark hugged her, feeling unequal for this discussion after a tiring day and a long flight. 'Tell you what, why doesn't Aunty Katie come home

again tonight and sleep with you?' Katie had
started this problem; she could at least help out
for another night. It might take her mind off her
five-year hopeless quest to make Simon look at
her—for a night, anyway.

Chloe promptly wiggled down to the ground
and bolted for the dining room. 'Aunty Katie,
Aunty Katie—you come sleep with Chloe
again!'

'You're only putting off the inevitable,' Sylvie
admonished him as she took his hand. 'But we can
put off this discussion until you've eaten and
slept.'

He looked at the upturned face of his beloved
wife, and once again felt deep thankfulness for
adorable stubbornness and impossible promises.
'Thanks, sweetheart.'

And they walked hand in hand into the dining
room of his parents' house, to the teasing laughter
and greetings of his loving family.

MILLS & BOON PUBLISH EIGHT LARGE PRINT TITLES A MONTH. THESE ARE THE EIGHT TITLES FOR FEBRUARY 2010.

DESERT PRINCE, BRIDE OF INNOCENCE
Lynne Graham

RAFFAELE: TAMING HIS TEMPESTUOUS VIRGIN
Sandra Marton

THE ITALIAN BILLIONAIRE'S SECRETARY MISTRESS
Sharon Kendrick

BRIDE, BOUGHT AND PAID FOR
Helen Bianchin

BETROTHED: TO THE PEOPLE'S PRINCE
Marion Lennox

THE BRIDESMAID'S BABY
Barbara Hannay

THE GREEK'S LONG-LOST SON
Rebecca Winters

HIS HOUSEKEEPER BRIDE
Melissa James

0210 Rom LP

MILLS & BOON PUBLISH EIGHT LARGE PRINT TITLES A MONTH. THESE ARE THE EIGHT TITLES FOR MARCH 2010.

A BRIDE FOR HIS MAJESTY'S PLEASURE
Penny Jordan

THE MASTER PLAYER
Emma Darcy

THE INFAMOUS ITALIAN'S SECRET BABY
Carole Mortimer

THE MILLIONAIRE'S CHRISTMAS WIFE
Helen Brooks

CROWNED: THE PALACE NANNY
Marion Lennox

CHRISTMAS ANGEL FOR THE BILLIONAIRE
Liz Fielding

UNDER THE BOSS'S MISTLETOE
Jessica Hart

JINGLE-BELL BABY
Linda Goodnight

millsandboon.co.uk Community

Join Us!

The Community is the perfect place to meet and chat to kindred spirits who love books and reading as much as you do, but it's also the place to:

- **Get the inside scoop from authors about their latest books**
- **Learn how to write a romance book with advice from our editors**
- **Help us to continue publishing the best in women's fiction**
- **Share your thoughts on the books we publish**
- **Befriend other users**

Forums: Interact with each other as well as authors, editors and a whole host of other users worldwide.

Blogs: Every registered community member has their own blog to tell the world what they're up to and what's on their mind.

Book Challenge: We're aiming to read 5,000 books and have joined forces with The Reading Agency in our inaugural Book Challenge.

Profile Page: Showcase yourself and keep a record of your recent community activity.

Social Networking: We've added buttons at the end of every post to share via digg, Facebook, Google, Yahoo, technorati and de.licio.us.

www.millsandboon.co.uk